CHALLENGING OFFER

"Where are you sleeping tonight?" she asked softly.

"Out near those new cut logs, more'n likely."

"No. Stay here with me."

"With you?"

"I don't want to sleep alone—not tonight."

"You got a short memory, ma'am."

She pulled back, suddenly contrite. "I know. I was dreadful to you that night. Now I want you to forgive me for what I said, how I acted. You must let me make amends."

He grinned at her and took his pipe out of his mouth. "When you put it like that, how's a man to refuse?"

And with that Kathleen flung her arms around his neck and drew him close to her. The heat of her body almost scalding him. . . .

GOLDEN HAWK 4

HELL'S CHILDREN

Will C. Knott

∅
A SIGNET BOOK

NEW AMERICAN LIBRARY

PUBLISHED BY
THE NEW AMERICAN LIBRARY
OF CANADA LIMITED

PUBLISHER'S NOTE

This book is a work of fiction. Names, characters, places, and incidents either are the product of the author's imagination or are used fictitiously, and any resemblance to actual persons, living or dead, events, or locales is entirely coincidental.

NAL BOOKS ARE AVAILABLE AT QUANTITY DISCOUNTS WHEN USED TO PROMOTE PRODUCTS OR SERVICES. FOR INFORMATION PLEASE WRITE TO PREMIUM MARKETING DIVISION, NEW AMERICAN LIBRARY, 1633 BROADWAY, NEW YORK, NEW YORK 10019.

First Printing, July, 1987

2 3   4   5   6   7   8   9

SIGNET TRADEMARK REG U S PAT OFF AND FOREIGN COUNTRIES
REGISTERED TRADEMARK — MARCA REGISTRADA
HECHO EN WINNIPEG CANADA

SIGNET, SIGNET CLASSIC, MENTOR, ONYX, PLUME, MERIDIAN AND NAL BOOKS are published in Canada by The New American Library of Canada, Limited, 81 Mack Avenue, Scarborough, Ontario, Canada M1L 1M8

PRINTED IN CANADA
COVER PRINTED IN U.S.A.

GOLDEN HAWK

A camp beside a quiet Texan stream. A sudden, fearsome cry . . . leaping savages . . . knives flashing . . . brutal, shameful death. . . .

Ripped from the bosom of their slain parents, carried off by Comanches, this hellish night under the glare of the Comanche moon is seared forever into the memories of Jed Thompson and his sister, Annabelle. His vengeance slaked at last, pursued relentlessly by his Comanche brothers, the plains and mountain tribesmen speak now in hushed tones of the terrible, unrelenting wrath of Golden Hawk.

Golden Hawk. Half white man, half Comanche. Mountain man. Pathfinder. Wagon master. Army scout. A legend in his own time. An awesome nemesis to his enemies. But a bulwark and a haven to those facing the terrors of that raw, savage land.

— 1 —

Golden Hawk was seeking a beaver stream that Yellowstone Kelly had assured him was just beyond these forested ridges. That was all he wanted. Just beaver. He was not looking for any trouble.

But of course, he realized, that was always when trouble came. Astride a powerful black stud, he had been pushing his mount carefully through thick timber when his senses told him he was being observed. Or followed. He pulled the stud to a halt. He was a tall, broad-shouldered hulk of a man dressed in fringed buckskin and boots, his untidy shock of blond hair mostly hidden by a black, wide-brimmed hat. His keen blue eyes peered out from under massive brows. His cheekbones were high, and the sharp blade of his nose resembled that of a bird of prey.

Hawk sat quietly, waiting, the stud swishing his tail impatiently. Traveling through the north-

7

ern fringes of Crow country meant they were pretty damn close to the Blackfoot Confederation's southern borders, and it was that time of year when the Blackfoot sometimes took it upon themselves to send raiders into Crow country to steal either Crow ponies or Crow women, whichever was handiest.

A blackbird called from a distance and Hawk heard the faint beat of wings. He remained as still as a rock, letting the feel of the timberland wash over him, acutely aware of its pungent abundance of fragrant grasses, firs, and sage, the small scurrying sound of tiny animals moving about in the brush, and the barely audible sigh of the wind moving through the tops of the pines.

Gradually Hawk became aware of a subtle diminution of sound—slight but noticeable. He glanced slowly, carefully around him. He saw nothing. But this did not mean a thing. The dense spruce and pine were close upon him. An army of savages could be lurking within twenty yards and not a single hide nor hair would show itself. The green, sunlit gleam of a small clearing caught his eye through the trees ahead of him and he nudged his stud toward it.

As soon as he broke through the timber, he sensed movement to his right. On the crest of a distant ridge, a Blackfoot warrior eased his war pony to a halt. There were two, three, four—finally seven Blackfoot warriors in all—a war party for sure. Buffalo capes over their shoulders, eagle feathers hanging from their lances, they sat quietly on their horses, watching him.

Though they were too far away for Hawk to catch the expression on their faces, he could tell from the arrogant arch of their backs that they had only contempt for this white-eyes below them.

Pretending that he regarded their sudden presence as no concern of his, Hawk nudged his horse forward and continued on across the small clearing. Not until he reentered the timber did he glance back. The Blackfoot were gone. That meant they were closer now than they had been a few minutes before. Spurring the stud to a lope, Hawk kept his head down and plunged through the timber, riding this time toward the distant, rushing sound of fast water, perhaps the very stream Yellowstone had described to him.

He broke out onto a buffalo trail that wound down through a timber-covered slope. He kept on it, and every second the roar of the water ahead of him grew louder. At last he caught, through the trees, the wink of sunlight on water. He left the buffalo trail and pushed through the timber until he found himself on a ridge high above a mountain stream so swift that its ebony surface was as smooth as glass. The sound of thundering water came from a waterfall farther downstream. Hawk could see the clouds of water vapor hanging in the air over the timber.

He turned his horse and started back to the buffalo trail when he found his way blocked by the Blackfoot warriors he had glimpsed earlier. Their stoic faces covered with war paint, they showed only a cruel indifference as they measured him for their scalping knives.

Suddenly one of the braves leaned close to his war chief and whispered something. The chief quickened. A short dialogue followed, and soon the entire war party came eagerly alive. When Hawk saw the quick gleam in their eyes—and the caution as well—he knew his identity had just been established. He was not just another foolish white face lost in Crow country and ripe for the picking.

He was Golden Hawk. And they *had* him!

Hawk could imagine what was going through their minds. They were thinking of their welcome when they returned to their village with the mighty Golden Hawk's scalp dangling from one of their coup sticks. An emissary would be sent far south to the Staked Plains to tell the Comanche of Golden Hawk's death—of this Blackfoot band's great victory over the killer of their people. In years hence, the tale of how they had slain Golden Hawk would be told over and over, each retelling gaining subtle yet wondrous embellishments.

To stall them, Hawk held up his hand in the traditional greeting of the plains and pulled the stud back a few steps until he was on the edge of the cliff. The Blackfoot did not return his salute. The war chief spoke to his companions, and at once two warriors raised their bows. They were already fitted with arrows. Swinging the stud around, Hawk kicked it out into space. As horse and rider plunged down toward the river, arrows snicked past them. The horse's bulk hit the river's surface with a powerful impact, throwing

Hawk clear. As the horse struggled against the powerful current in an effort to reach the far shore, Hawk took after it.

Above the fall's ominous roar, Hawk heard a sharp war cry coming from high above. He glanced up and saw a naked Blackfoot, armed only with a hatchet, leaping after him. He knifed into the water less than twenty feet away, reappeared almost instantly, and began swimming furiously toward Hawk, who turned at once to meet him.

He took a few quick strokes, then dived deeper into the water's icy embrace. So cold was the water that the shock of it nearly closed off his lungs. Brushing the bottom of the stream for a moment, he twisted about, then pulled himself up toward the dim light shimmering far above him. He could see the Blackfoot warrior splashing about on the surface, waiting for him. As he shot up toward the unsuspecting warrior, the swift current caught him. Only by redoubling his efforts was he able to gain the surface. As his head broke free of the water, he found himself only a few feet from the waiting Blackfoot. The savage's dark eyes shone with eagerness as he lunged toward Hawk. His hatchet sliced down, glancing off Hawk's shoulder. Gulping in a huge swallow of air, Hawk dived once again, kicking frantically down through the icy water. Abruptly, he twisted about and shot for the surface.

But the Blackfoot was ready for him this time, kicking down through the water toward him. He no longer had a hatchet. Instead, a long blade gleamed in the dull light. Hawk kicked himself backward, dived, tumbled completely around, and came up with his bowie flashing. The Blackfoot tried to evade his thrust, but was not fast enough. Hawk's blade sliced into his right thigh, opening a long gash clear to his ankle. Ignoring his wound, the Blackfoot kicked around and came at Hawk again.

Blood trailing behind him like a great dark rope, the Indian slashed a bite out of Hawk's left shoulder. But Hawk did not retreat. As his opponent swept past him, Hawk thrust up again with his bowie. This time its blade sank deep into the warrior's chest under his breastbone. As the Blackfoot's momentum swept him beyond Hawk, the blade slit the brave open from his brisket clear to his belly button. As the emptying body plunged past him, Hawk almost lost his blade. In a moment the Indian vanished, his lifeless, tumbling form lost in the dark penumbra of blood flowing like billowing smoke from his wounds.

His own lungs nearly bursting, Hawk paddled for the surface, broke it, and found himself in the midst of a tremendous, gut-wrenching roar. Glancing toward the sound, he saw, about fifty yards ahead of him, the tight, gleaming surface of the water as it vanished into the gorge beyond. The undertow had him by this time, and he struggled desperately to swim out of its grasp. But he was exhausted and realized it was futile to struggle against the current.

He did the only thing he could. He gave in to the relentless flow, lowered his head, and paddled frantically toward the waterfall. His heart sank as he saw just ahead of him the clean edge of the swift water plunging over the edge. For an instant he glimpsed the mountain slopes beyond the gorge, their flanks mantled with pine and spruce. Then he was swept headlong over the edge. He did his best to launch himself as far as he could out from the base of the fall.

Though he succeeded in missing the boulder-strewn area just beneath the falls, as he glanced down he saw almost directly beneath him a great shattered chunk of a boulder thrusting up out of the frothing waters. Somehow he managed to slip to one side and slice off it, plunging deep into the foaming water beyond it. The pounding water caught at him and pulled him still deeper. He was knocked about like a rag doll and felt himself glance off one submerged boulder, only to slam into another. When his head broke the surface at last, he saw another boulder rushing toward him. Reaching out, he grabbed it, clinging to its edge. The broken stone cut cruelly into his chest and thigh, but he hung on grimly and let the wild waters flow over and around him until he had regained enough strength to enable him to clamber up onto the boulder.

He was at the near side of the gorge, a great, shelving arm of rock shielding him from any who might be peering down from above. Wincing against the shuddering, insistent roar of the cataract, Hawk glanced up through the mists at the edge of the falls, half-expecting to see another Blackfoot plunging after him. But of course none came. The rest of the war party, having seen

Hawk swept over the falls, would assume he was dead.

They had every reason to believe so. Only good luck had kept Hawk alive.

A quick inspection showed the long, clawlike abrasion reaching from his shoulder to his thigh, the mark left by the boulder as he glanced off it. His entire side ached some, and additional bruises covered his body from the battering he took when he was swept among the rocks. His shoulder wound had been washed clean by the cold water and was now bleeding steadily, sending a thin, pale flow down over his chest; but no muscles or nerves had been severed, and as Hawk stood up to gaze around him, he realized that though he might be a little bent, he was not yet broken.

The dead Blackfoot had preceded him over the falls and now lay in a shallows not twenty feet away. He was little more than a broken piece of flesh, barely recognizable as a human being. Alongside him, curiously enough, lay Hawk's hat, caught in a shallows. Hawk splashed over to it through the icy water and swung the hat repeatedly to rid it of some of its moisture, then placed the cold crown down over his head.

The stud had not survived his trip over the falls. He lay on the far side of the stream close by the bank, crushed between two boulders, his head in the water, the swift current tugging at it. Stepping from boulder to boulder, Hawk made his way across the stream to the dead animal and found that, though his pistol and rifle were soaked through, the pistol was still mechanically sound and the rifle's heavy, octagonal barrel was not bent, its stock still solidly attached.

Soaked thoroughly were his powder horn and powder, meaning that for now he would have to rely on his knives—the bowie and his throwing knife. Lifting his saddle and the rest of his gear off the dead horse was a long, tedious chore, and it was close to sundown when he left the stream and made a dry, fireless camp deep in the timber. He needed a fire to dry him and his buckskins, but the mountains were alive with Blackfoot, he realized, and this time there would be no waterfall to save him. He spent the night fitfully, his long, powerful frame trembling in the mountain's chill embrace.

With morning came a sun bright enough to warm him, but it did nothing for the relentless aching of his body, the result of the battering he had taken when he went over the falls. His shoulder wound was no longer bleeding, however, and after burying his saddle and blazing a nearby spruce as a marker, he set out through the timber.

He was almost certain he had been close to finding that stream filled with beaver when the Blackfoot came upon him, but what he wanted now was shelter, a place to hole up until he could steal a new mount for himself, something he would obtain from the next party of Blackfeet he came upon. He made himself that promise.

That night he found an abandoned bear den. The stench of the mother bear and her cubs was still strong, but it was no hindrance to him and soon enough he fell into a deep, healing sleep.

*   *   *

A week later, fully recovered from his plunge over the falls, Hawk stopped in his tracks, alerted by the ominous pop of faint gunfire: three, perhaps, four shots came first, then a flurry, which lasted only a few minutes; a second flurry followed, and after that ... silence.

The forest around Hawk had grown ominously quiet. Even the finch over his head lost heart. Hawk started walking again and pushed on through the depressing stillness, waiting for the sound of more gunfire to give him direction. When it came, he shifted slightly south and continued on, trotting now steadily, tirelessly, the steady exertion darkening his buckskins with sweat and easing the ache he had felt since morning.

He continued on without the benefit of further gunfire to guide him, heading southwest until he came out onto a spur overlooking a broad valley. Enclosed by a range of towering mountains, it was about thirty miles long and at least three or four miles wide. The length and breadth of it was watered by a placid, meandering stream.

Almost directly below him, a wagon train had halted next to a field of giant boulders. One ox had been slain and remained where it had fallen. The remaining oxen stood placidly, cropping the grass at their feet. The only sign of the settlers was movement in and around the wagons and shifts of color in the brush around them. No Indians were in sight. They were probably lying low, Hawk realized, waiting for nightfall before pressing home their attack.

The valley's floor was a good distance below Hawk. He examined the timbered slope and judged that even if he moved down through it at the greatest speed possible, it would still take close to three hours before he reached the wagons, perhaps longer. Two vast outcroppings of rock protruded from the slope, each one presenting a formidable barrier to anyone attempting to proceed beyond them to the valley floor.

Hawk took a deep breath and seriously considered moving on, leaving the settlers to their own devices. More than likely they would survive if they stuck together and used their firepower judiciously. All they had to do was make the Indians pay too dear a price for the wagons. Like children reaching for a pie on a windowsill, they would take these wagons only as long as the deed could be accomplished without severe retaliation. Otherwise, they would pass by this prize.

The crack of a dried twig underfoot caused Hawk to turn his head. A tall, buckskin-clad figure stepped out of the brush and confronted Hawk warily. He was close to six foot seven with gaunt features, and was so lanky that his bony wrists seemed to hang a mile out of his sleeves. Though he was more scarecrow than man, Hawk sensed a rawhide strength about him, something akin to the burnished toughness of a hickory stick.

Over one shoulder rested a full saddlebag and over the other a bedroll. He carried an ancient flintlock rifle that had been altered to fire with a percussion lock. He also packed a long skinning knife, and stuck in his belt were a war hatchet and a breech-loading percussion pistol. So Hawk would not misunderstand his intent, he was careful not to lift the rifle barrel as he came to a halt.

"Howdy," Hawk said, turning to face the man squarely.

The fellow grinned slyly. "Been watchin' you, hoss. Reckon you're tryin' to decide if you should go down there to help them pilgrims."

"And if I am, just who might you be?"

"Some call me Long Tom. That ain't my name, but it fits me well enough. I've already noted the color of your hair. So you don't have to tell me who *you* are."

Hawk made no effort to deny who he was.

Long Tom indicated the wagons pulled up in the valley below them with a quick jerk of his head. "You decided what to do about them yet?"

"Like you said, I been thinkin' on it. Looks like a big-enough wagon train to take care of themselves."

"They are rank green pilgrims, hoss. And that's a mean bees' nest of hungry Bannocks out lookin' for easy pickin's."

"Bannock? I expected they'd be Blackfoot."

"Oh, there's Blackfoot about. I ain't denyin' that, hoss. They're thicker than fleas on a hound dog in these here mountains. And more on the way."

"You know this for sure, do you?"

His smile was big and friendly. "Hoss, there ain't much happens in these mountains I don't know about."

"So what do you suggest we do about those pilgrims below us?"

"Suit yourself, hoss. But I figure it wouldn't be Christian to let them Bannocks get away with all them goods and all them white women—even if their men folks *were* silly enough to bring them out here in the first place."

"That means you're suggesting we go on down there and even the odds some. That it?"

"I don't see we got much of a choice."

"Then we'd better get moving."

Long Tom lit his pipe. "Just wait awhile, hoss. We don't need to be in any big hurry. I figure the Bannocks are waitin' for dark before they move on them wagons again."

"It'll take us that long to get down there."

"No, it won't. I know a quick trail down. But there's no way we can take a horse over it. We'll have to go on foot."

"That don't matter. I don't have a horse."

"I noticed. Mine, I left back in my cabin, a good two days' march from here." Long Tom finished tamping fresh tobacco into the bowl of his clay pipe, then sat cross-legged before a tree and lit up. "As I told you before, we got plenty of time," he said, puffing contentedly.

Irritated slightly, Hawk dropped his saddlebags and other gear to the ground beside a tree, sat down, and leaned back against it. The moment his head touched the tree, four painted Blackfoot warriors burst out of the brush not ten yards from them.

Long Tom's hatchet caught the closest Blackfoot

in the center of his forehead, cleaving it neatly. The second warrior took a round from Long Tom's rifle and plunged to his knees, both hands trying to hold in his exploded gut. Hawk was on his feet by this time. Reaching back, he sent his throwing knife at the third Blackfoot, the blade lodging in his throat. The fourth warrior, now only a few feet from Long Tom, took a ball in his chest from Tom's pistol. Tom ducked aside as the warrior tumbled dazedly past him and collapsed in the brush behind the tree.

As quickly as it had begun, it was over.

Long Tom grinned over at Hawk. "I knew they were comin'," he admitted, somewhat sheepishly. "But I didn't want to say anything. Wanted you to act real natural, like you and me didn't expect a thing. Surest way to draw them in."

"Wasn't that taking quite a chance?"

"Hell's fire, not with Golden Hawk on my side, it wasn't."

"You sure that's all of them?"

"I counted four comin' after you."

"There might be more you missed."

"Don't look like it to me, Hawk," he said, glancing around him at the awesome carnage.

Hawk shrugged. This fellow was a wild one, for sure. He didn't know if it would be very safe traveling with a man who took those kinds of chances. But he said nothing.

Long Tom knocked the unsmoked tobacco out of his clay pipe and dropped it into his saddlebag, then stood up. "Ready?" he asked Hawk.

Hawk walked over to the Blackfoot he had

stopped with his throwing knife. The Indian was dead. Hawk removed his knife and wiped the blade off on the Blackfoot's greasy hair. "I'm ready."

"Like you just said, the trail down to the valley can be tricky," Long Tom warned as they started off. "There's a devil's own acre of loose shale and talus near the foot of this slope and a big outcropping of rock halfway down. So just follow me close."

Ignoring the dead and dying Blackfoot scattered about on the grass of the small clearing, Long Tom stepped past Hawk and moved into the forest. Hawk followed. A few minutes later they came to a narrow game trail and Long Tom followed it down a steep, timbered slope.

So familiar was he with the trail, the tall woodsman was soon at least ten yards ahead of Hawk and was just passing a clump of white pine when Hawk thought he saw a wolf leap upon him. Too many trees were between them for Hawk to be certain. Dropping his saddlebags, he raced down the slope and saw it was not a wolf, but a Blackfoot warrior attacking Long Tom.

Letting out a chilling war cry, the warrior raised his knife and brought it down in a great, slashing arc. Tom managed somehow to reach up and parry the Blackfoot's knife thrust with the handle of his hatchet. The two slashed wildly, futilely at each other for a moment; then, locked in a deadly embrace, they went tumbling down the slope, through brush and over downed limbs, until they came to a sudden, jolting halt against the base of a huge boulder. Long Tom got the worst of it, his back slamming into the boulder, the Blackfoot on top. The wind knocked out of him, too dazed to fight back, Tom let his hatchet fall to the ground as he stared slackly up at the Blackfoot. Once again the savage lifted his knife, ready to plunge it into Long Tom's chest.

Close enough by that time, Hawk flung himself headlong, catching the Indian about the waist and pulling him down the slope beyond the boulder. Fully spent by this time, the Indian nevertheless put up a determined struggle until Hawk managed to club him nearly senseless with the butt of his pistol. He twisted the warrior's knife from his grasp. Positioning himself on top of the Blackfoot's chest, Hawk pinned both arms with his knees, drew his bowie, and thrust quickly, breaking the skin of the warrior's throat. He was about to finish the business with one ear-to-ear slash when the dazed Blackfoot abruptly stopped struggling.

Unable to slash the throat of a man no longer struggling, Hawk pulled back slightly. The warrior's eyes opened. They were great, dark, fathomless orbs. As they gazed full into Hawk's eyes, their unblinking intensity resembled those of a wild animal rather than an Indian's.

"To die at the hands of Golden Hawk will not shame me," the Blackfoot told Hawk gravely, speaking in poor but passable Comanche. "Only do not cleave the head of Wolf Heart from his body. Let him pass into the Land of the Shadows a whole man, able to ride with those warriors who have gone before him."

Hawk's knife was still pressing against the Indian's throat. To the Blackfoot, Hawk knew, the world after this one was a place called the Sandhills, a grim land where the souls of the departed endured a shadowy existence that was only a mockery of earthly life. But it was a life hereafter nevertheless, and if Hawk severed this Blackfoot's head from his shoulders, his belief was that his shadow would be doomed to wander forever between this world and the next.

Glancing up the slope, Hawk saw that though Long Tom was still slumped against the rock, he was beginning to regain consciousness and would probably be all right. Hawk looked back down at Wolf Heart and addressed him in Comanche.

"Is this the last of your war party?"

Wolf Heart nodded.

"You speak the Comanche tongue, yet you are a Blackfoot."

"Like you, I was taken by the Comanches when I was a cub. I too escaped and returned to my father's people."

"Who are your people?"

"My people are the Bloods, my band those of the White Lodges. This land is ours. We will not share it with the Crows or the Bannocks—or even the terrible Golden Hawk."

Though there was something ominous about this warrior beneath him, Hawk could not help but admire his courage. The fact that he too had been a captive of the Comanches made him seem almost a brother under the skin. Hawk decided he could not kill him.

"You are a brave warrior," Hawk told the Blackfoot. "As are all the Blackfoot. I would let you live. But if you are too proud to accept life as the gift of Golden Hawk, I will understand and plunge this blade into your heart and leave your head on your shoulders. Then you may journey to the Sandhills and join the shadows of your dead. Tell me what you wish."

"This warrior will accept his life as the gift of Golden Hawk."

Hawk sheathed his bowie. "Done," he said, standing up.

— 2 —

Long Tom was on his feet, staring down the slope at Hawk.

"What in hell you doin', Hawk?" he demanded.

"What does it look like?"

"You just let that hell's spawn go free!"

Hawk walked back up the slope to Long Tom. "Yes, I did."

"He near killed me!"

"But he didn't. I saw to that."

Long Tom looked soberly at Hawk and scratched the back of his head. "I guessed maybe you did stop him at that. You saved my life."

"Looks that way."

Long Tom's hard, lean face broke into a grin. He shrugged his coat-hanger shoulders. "Well, then, I have no cause for complaint."

"That's real decent of you."

"I just hope you don't regret lettin' that red

devil go," he said solemnly, wincing slightly as he rubbed the back of his head.

A slight grin broke Hawk's craggy face. "I probably will regret it," he admitted. "You still up to facin' those Bannocks?"

"Hell, yes!"

Long Tom picked up his hatchet and went back up the slope to fetch his rifle and pistol along with his pack and saddlebags, all of which had gone flying when Wolf Heart attacked him. Hawk went back up the slope with him to regain the saddlebags and gear he had dropped, after which the two men continued on down through the timber, still following the game trail.

On the brow of a great white outcropping of rock, it petered out, and their progress from then on was exceedingly dangerous as they found themselves at times picking their way across rock faces so smooth they offered little or no opportunity for hand or footholds. Close to the valley floor they were confronted with steep washes filled with gravel and later with slopes slippery with shale and talus. At times their footing was so uncertain that they were slowed almost to a crawl. By the time they reached the valley floor, it was close to sundown.

Though they could not be certain, they judged the stalled wagons to be at least a mile farther along the valley floor. From where they stood, the wagons were not visible, but since they knew the wagons had pulled up close under the canyon wall near a field of boulders, they sighted the tops of the tallest boulders and set out. It was almost completely dark when they reached the boulder field. Hawk glanced up at the sky. The day had been overcast and there was not a single star showing. This promised to be a black, moonless night.

Moving on through the boulder field toward the wagons, they were stopped by a sharp, icy command: "Hold it right there!"

The voice came out of the darkness just ahead of them. Both men halted. A match scratched, then flared to their right, and a second later a lantern was held up in front of them while an enclosing ring of settlers peered intently at them.

The settler holding the lantern was as tall as Hawk. A dark beard covered his face, and his eyes gleamed with malice as well as astonishment. The rest of the settlers—all of them packing firearms—seemed just as surprised if not as belligerent.

"Get that damn light out of my face," Hawk said, pushing the lantern away.

"We came to help," explained Long Tom.

"Help? You two?"

"We heard the gunfire from the ridge above."

A smaller man stepped up alongside the black-bearded one. His look and manner were entirely different. Stocky of build, with shoulders that would have been comfortable on a blacksmith, he had a round, clean-shaven face and a quick smile.

Snatching the offending lantern from his companion, he smiled warmly at Hawk and Long

Tom. "Welcome! You're right. We did have trouble earlier. We're much obliged to you for coming down here to help us. But you came for nothin', looks like. Them redskins have not shown hide nor hair since we opened up on them."

"That don't mean a thing," cautioned Long Tom. "The Bannocks are a shifty, cunning lot. They won't give up that easy, less'n you killed a passel of them."

"No, I don't think we killed many," said the man. "Though we certainly expended a great deal of shot and powder." Smiling then, he stuck out his hand. "Excuse me for not introducing myself," he said, shaking each of their hands in turn. "I am Justin Martin, the duly elected leader of this wagon train."

Long Tom introduced himself and Hawk gave his Christian name, Jed Thompson. The other members of the wagon train shuffled awkwardly forward and introduced themselves also. The one with the full beard called himself John Barley and introduced himself as the second in command of the wagon train, appearing to be inordinately fond of holding his mouth in a straight, grim line as he peered intently at those he addressed.

"Where are you headed?" Hawk asked Justin Martin.

"Oregon Territory."

"Where you from?"

"New England—Vermont, to be exact."

"You've come a long way," acknowledged Long Tom.

"And where might you hail from, Long Tom?"

"Cambridge, Massachusetts. I taught biology at Harvard for a while."

"Harvard?" Justin Martin gasped. "You must be joking, man!"

"I am not joking. Teaching was a dull, tedious business, and I am glad to be a free man in this wilderness. Not having had to wear a tie for seven years, I count myself a very fortunate man."

Every settler there was immensely impressed, but Hawk caught skepticism in some eyes. He did not know much about the East, and had no idea why teaching at a place called Harvard should have raised so many eyebrows. He decided that when the time came, he'd ask Long Tom about it.

The formalities concluded, Hawk and Long Tom were led through the darkness to the wagons. There were fourteen in all, many more than had been visible from the ridge above, and they had been wisely drawn into a circle. Stepping over a pair of traces and entering the clearing within, Hawk saw that the women were busy feeding a huge fire, over which—on a hastily contrived spit—they were slowly turning the ox that the attacking Bannocks had killed. The entire encampment was redolent with the mouth-watering aroma of roasting beef.

"My God," Long Tom remarked to Hawk anxiously, "a scent like that hanging on the wind would be enough to draw the devil himself."

"You better put out that fire," Hawk told Martin.

"Why?"

"It's sure as hell givin' them Bannocks a reason for trying again."

"What Bannocks?" John Barley demanded. "We already told you. We drove them off."

"That's right," Justin Martin agreed. "I truly believe we have. And we haven't eaten since noon. I say we're due a modest celebration, at least. You men are welcome to join us, of course."

"You won't eat again if you don't douse those flames," Hawk insisted.

"I know the Bannocks," Long Tom said, gently but forcefully. "They are right now priming themselves for another attack. This wagon train is too great an attraction for them to let it go without at least one more attempt to take it. It's just about dark enough right now for them to try again."

"Nonsense," said John Barley. "We're more than a match for them naked aborigines, and they know it."

Justin Martin nodded his agreement, but before he could say anything, an arrow whipped out of the darkness and plunged into his chest. Pure astonishment on his face, he sank to the ground, made a feeble effort to pluck the arrow from his heart, then pitched forward onto the ground. He was dead before he struck it.

Instantly, the night was filled with the cries of attacking Bannocks. Erupting from the darkness beyond the wagons, they hopped lightly over the wagons' traces and poured into the compound, their faces painted hideously, their shrieks enough to freeze the blood in a man's veins. But the settlers were game. They stood their ground and sent a punishing fusilade at the attackers. Hawk saw two warriors topple to the ground, then another. Immediately, the rest broke ranks and dispersed into the shadows about the wagons.

Meanwhile, screaming in terror, the women fled their nearly roasted ox on the spit and ran frantically for the wagons. Before they reached them, a Bannock arrow caught one of the women in the back. Crying out, she stumbled, then sprawled facedown, the arrow sticking straight up out of her back. Before Hawk or Long Tom could warn him, the woman's husband raced out from the cover of the wagons. Before he could reach her, an arrow buried itself in his side. He cried out once, and as he dropped to the ground, a second arrow silenced him.

Crouched in the shadows between two wagons, Hawk fired at a skulking shadow and heard the Indian's muffled cry. As he reloaded swiftly, beside him Long Tom fired at another shadowy figure—with similar results.

"Damn," Tom exclaimed impatiently. "Maybe we should've stayed out of this."

Hawk nodded gloomily. "I've been thinking the same thing."

Suddenly two mounted Bannocks, filling the air with their savage cries, galloped through the ring of wagons into the clearing and lashed their mounts toward the campfire. As they swept closer to it, the settlers opened a murderous fire on them. The two savages were not deterred. Riding boldly through the curtain of fire, the first Bannock dropped a rope over the head of the roasting ox, yanked him away from the fire—spit and all—then rode back the way he had come, dragging the smoking carcass after him.

The second warrior rode boldly, swiftly through the fire, scattering its embers with his horse's hooves, then took after his companion. Both warriors seemed to bear a charmed life as the volley of fire from the wagons caught nothing vital. For a breathless moment, the ox's hind end got caught against a wagon's traces. The second Bannock leapt off his horse and heaved it over the traces. Their triumphant cries filling the night, the two Indians rode away, dragging their succulent prize after them.

For a second or two there was only silence. Then came the screams and sobbing of the women—a fearsome outcry. But the attack was not over, Hawk realized as he and Long Tom moved in under a wagon and lay prone on the damp grass, peering out through the spokes of the wagon's wheels. While Hawk watched the area within the ring of wagons, Long Tom peered out in the direction of the boulder field. Hawk and Long Tom had no doubt that the Bannocks were still out there, resting up, allowing the dark, impenetrable shadows of the moonless night to cloak them.

Huddled in the wagon over their heads was

Justin Martin's widow, Hawk realized. A woman companion was doing her best to comfort her, but the bereaved woman was close to hysteria. Hawk realized that without their leader, the settlers were in trouble even if they did manage to fight off the Bannocks.

Lying there on the grass, Hawk realized he could still smell the roasting oxen. Portions of its succulent hide had evidently fallen off as it was being dragged across the grass. He sniffed at it greedily, his stomach roiling. Then he had an idea. He glanced over his shoulder at Long Tom.

"Can you smell that?"

"I can," Tom answered.

"Would you be thinking what I'm thinking?"

"I am. That ox was cooked almost clear through."

"And them Bannocks are probably having themselves a real feast right about now."

Long Tom nodded, looked back out at the shadowy field of boulders, saying nothing for a while. Then he remarked softly, "Hard to believe—them two Bannocks showin' such courage, riding in here like that."

"As bold as brass."

"Of course, once they finish up that ox, they'll be right back here to continue the fun."

"No doubt about it," Golden Hawk agreed.

"I say we don't wait."

Hawk frowned. "You mean, leave these here fool pilgrims to their fate?"

"Now, you know we can't do that, Hawk."

"Sure I know it. So what're you suggesting?"

"That we join them Bannocks at that feast. It ain't polite of them to take all that beef and not invite us. Downright impolite, I say—and me as hungry as a bear in springtime."

In the dim light from the fire's remaining embers, Hawk saw Long Tom's grin. It was wolfish. "Lead on, Tom"—Hawk chuckled—"I'm game."

Hawk crawled out past the wagon wheel, stood up, and peered into the canvas-covered interior of the wagon. He could barely make out the pale face of the woman he had heard comforting the widow. She was sitting up against a pillow, her waves of uncombed dark hair nearly covering it.

When she gasped in fear at the sight of Hawk's head and shoulders looming in the canvas opening, he spoke swiftly to reassure her. "Tom and I are going to do some scouting, see if maybe we can find where the Bannocks are. We won't be long."

"Good luck," the woman said softly.

Her low, seductive voice stirred something deep within Hawk, and he wished for a moment that he could see her face more clearly. But there was no time for lingering. He turned away from the ring of wagons and headed out toward the field of boulders, Long Tom at his side.

They cleared the boulder-strewn field without incident and found themselves in a marshy lowland. Before long they were wading across a wide, low-banked stream toward the glow of a distant campfire that appeared to be coming from the far bank, beyond a thick clump of timber. Just as they had hoped! The Bannocks had built a fire and were finishing up that roasted ox.

Grinning, Hawk glanced at Long Tom. "Looks like we guessed right."

"And with them gorgin' themselves, they'll be no fit warriors, I'm thinking."

"For sure they won't be at their best."

Before they reached the timber, the two men separated in order to circle into it singly, coming at the Bannocks' fire from opposite directions. Their plan was to give each other plenty of time to make their approach. When Hawk opened fire, that would be the signal for Long Tom to join in.

Now, peering at the Indian encampment through a thick clump of brush, Hawk estimated that he was not more than forty yards from the fire and the Bannocks sitting cross-legged around it. Still in their war paint, the savages were tearing at the roasted meat like ravenous wolves. Some portions of the oxen had not been thoroughly roasted, but this made no difference as all of it was devoured greedily by the savages, red blood streaming down their chins, forearms, and bared chests.

It reminded Hawk of his days with the Comanches. After the summer buffalo hunt, the triumphant hunters would leap from their horses, disembowel the great, shaggy beasts they had just slain, and devour their livers, tearing at the steaming organs with keen teeth while fresh, red blood covered their faces and shoulders, the gory mess streaming over their sweaty torsos clear down to their breechclouts.

Hawk raised his rifle and sighted on the back

of the nearest Bannock, one who was tearing with his teeth at one such barely singed morsel. The round caught him in the back of the head, flinging him forward into the fire. As the sparks leapt up, Long Tom opened up from the other side of the clearing. Another Bannock dropped. Crabbing sideways, Hawk used his pistol on the next warrior who charged toward him.

Hawk went back to his Plains rifle. Loading it as any good Comanche hunter would in the midst of a buffalo chase, he kept three to four balls in his mouth, dumped powder into the muzzle, then spat a ball into it. Careful not to lower the muzzle too far before firing, he was able to loose a deadly hail of lead at the Bannocks.

Caught between Hawk's fire and that of Long Tom's, the Bannocks deserted their roast ox and broke for cover, disappearing swiftly into the timber. At once, Hawk and Long Tom raced out to the fire, snatching up well-cooked chunks of oxen and stuffing them into their shirtfronts. Then, to make sure the Bannocks would dine no more on the stolen meat, they urinated thoroughly over the steaming carcass, almost putting out the fire in the process.

Racing back into the timber, they headed for the wagons as fast as the moonless night would allow. At times they could hear the unmistakable sound of Indians crashing through the darkness around them, but they kept going. Only after they reached the other side of the stream and were wading heavily through the marshland did two Bannocks catch up with them. One shadowy warrior emerged from a clump of alder on dry ground just ahead of Hawk. The other one splashed up behind them. He ran with a fixed, dogged determination across the wet, uneven ground of the marsh, a gleaming dagger in his hand.

Hawk had reloaded his pistol as he ran. Raising it almost casually, he sent a round into the Bannock coming at him from the alders. The round caught the warrior in the chest and stopped him in his tracks. As Hawk gained the embankment and swept past him, he severed the Bannock's jugular with a single, terrible slash of his bowie. Turning then, he saw Long Tom send a round from his rifle into the Bannock closing on them from behind. Wounded fatally, the savage plunged forward for two more strides before stumbling facedown into the shallow water.

A moment later the two men reached the comparative safety of the boulder field. Not long after, they reached the wagons and found the settlers still huddled in the darkness between one of the wagons, John Barley doing all the talking, the frightened women huddled behind him, listening intently.

As soon as they reached the settlers, John Barley turned to confront them. "I am convinced the aborigines have fled," he stated flatly. "We have them on the run. Obviously, all they wanted was food, and that roasted oxen satisfied them."

Both men casually took out of their shirts the meat they had rescued from the Bannocks' campfire, and began eating. The surprise on the settlers' faces made it all worthwhile. Long Tom wiped his mouth with the back of his hand and grinned at John Barley.

"That roasted oxen will give them little pleasure now," Long Tom said, grinning. "Not in the condition we left it."

"The Bannocks have not fled," Hawk told Barley. "They were pressing us pretty damn close when we reached that boulder field out there. I suggest you disperse at once and guard your wagons."

"You were wrong before, Barley," Long Tom said. "They weren't gone then—and they're still out there now. This is going to be a long night. You'd better prepare for trouble."

"Nonsense!"

"Wait a minute," said one of the settlers, stepping between John Barley and Hawk. He was a short redhead with fiery blue eyes and a splash of freckles across his youthful face. "John, if this feller says we got to prepare for trouble, I say we better listen to him."

"Angus, may I remind you that I am now the leader of this wagon train?"

"And may I remind you that I have a fortune in store goods that I'll need if I am to set up in business when we get to Oregon? If we're not careful, these heathen barbarians will be trading my goods all over this wilderness. I say we listen to these two mountain men. They certainly know their way about in these parts."

A mutter of agreement swept over the settlers who had crowded around. One of the women, her warm, dark eyes resting fully on Hawk, spoke out clearly, "I say listen to Angus, or we'll all die here at the hands of these aborigines."

The rest of the women nodded vigorously.

Hawk recognized the woman's voice at once. It was she who had been comforting Justin Martin's widow, the one he had spoken to before setting out after the Bannocks.

"That settles it, then," said Angus. He turned to Hawk. "From now on, it looks like we're in your hands. We'll let you take us out of this."

John Barley fairly exploded. "Now, see here, Angus! Who elected you to be our spokesman?"

"I just did," said Angus. He turned to the rest of the settlers then. "What say the rest of you?" he asked.

There was a hearty, unmistakable shout of agreement.

John Barley spun around and stalked off toward his wagon.

Angus looked grimly at Hawk and Long Tom. "That wasn't very democratic, I admit, but you two are now officially in charge."

"You didn't ask us," reminded Long Tom. "Seems to me, you'd be the best one to lead this bunch. You sure as hell have the balls for it."

"Later, perhaps," Angus admitted. "But right now, it is your skill as woodsmen and your knowledge of these aborigines that we are relying on to help carry us through this."

"We ain't goin' all the way to Oregon, hoss," warned Long Tom.

"Of course not. Just help us now if you will," Angus said.

Long Tom looked at Hawk and shrugged. He obviously saw no harm in that.

"Fine," said Angus. "Now we had better do as you suggested earlier—see to our wagons and get ready for another attack."

As the men streamed off, Hawk and Long Tom slumped down on the grass, leaned back against a wagon wheel, and began reloading their weapons. It was not an easy business in the darkness, but long practice had made them experts at the task. From the wagons around them came the sounds of men moving about briskly, shifting trunks, leading off horses, dropping tailgates— doing what they could to prepare them and their loved ones for the assault they expected soon. Meanwhile, from many of the wagons came muffled sobbing and weeping. For the most part, the women were terrified, and no amount of rough comfort from their menfolk seemed capable of calming them.

The tall woman who had spoken up earlier materialized out of the darkness and strode toward them. She was a strikingly handsome woman. Though her bosom was full, she had a waist almost small enough for Hawk to enclose with his hands. Her shock of hair was as dark as night, her pale neck long and graceful. What really got Hawk's blood up, however, was the pouting fullness of her lips—the lower one especially.

"I am Kathleen MacLennan," she told them, her dark eyes resting on Hawk boldly. "Angus is my brother. He thinks it would be a good idea if you two helped Justin Martin's widow and myself with her wagon, and saw to our safety." She smiled. "I think it's a good idea, too."

"Of course," Hawk said, getting to his feet.

"We'd be delighted," seconded Long Tom.

"Good," Kathleen said. "I'll show you the way to our wagon."

Turning, she led them to the same wagon under which they had crouched earlier. This time, they noticed, someone had placed a blanket and a pillow under the wagon.

"Better if we don't sleep, ma'am," Long Tom told her. "Not while we're keepin' watch."

"I understand that, Long Tom. The blanket is there to keep off the chill. This ground's pretty damp."

"There's only one blanket."

"Then perhaps Jed could sleep up in the wagon off the ground, and you could stay under the wagon and keep watch. There's no sense in both of you getting a cold from this damp ground."

Long Tom looked at Hawk, doing his best to keep his astonishment from showing. "Why, sure," he said. "That's a fine idea. Go ahead, Hawk. I'll stay out here and keep my eyes peeled."

"Thanks, Tom." Hawk reached up and hauled himself into the back of the covered wagon.

Kathleen, hiking her big skirt, followed in after him. A heavy blanket had been strung across the center of the wagon, and on the other side of it, Hawk could hear a woman snoring, the Widow Martin, he realized.

He turned. Kathleen was so close behind him that he found himself holding on to her to keep his balance. That was all it took. She flung off her skirt and blouse, then her corset and chemise, and crouched beside him completely nude, her taut, sleek body aflame to his touch.

Embracing him with an intensity that bespoke long nights of sheer need, she drew him down beside her onto her already made bed. But sleep was the last thing on her mind. Yanking urgently at his buckskin britches, she peeled them off with a wantonness that thoroughly aroused Hawk.

It had been a long time for him, too.

Her lips brushing his right ear, she warned him to be as quiet as he could, so as not to disturb Hester Martin sleeping on the other side of the blanket, or Long Tom below them under the wagon.

He chuckled softly. "This here isn't something you can do quietly."

But she was not listening. Kissing him on the lips, she pulled him over on top of her. "I may be dead before morning," she told him, her voice shaking with emotion, "but I'm going to have myself a man before I go—or before I give it away to them damn heathens out there."

All of a sudden, it seemed, he was aroused as he had never been before. Something in the wild improbability of this coupling—in the fact that it was taking place under the most dangerous of circumstances—set him afire.

Aware that she was ready—more than ready,

in fact—he thrust into her and heard her tiny gasp of delight as he plunged so deep as to strike bottom. Her fingers became claws digging into his shoulders, and her mouth worked frantically as he began thrusting urgently, heedlessly, pounding her buttocks rhythmically against the bottom of the wagon.

Abruptly, caught up in Hawk's violent frenzy, she flung her arms around his neck and began to pant quickly, urgently, her arms threatening to cut off his breath, she held him so tightly. He passed the point of no return, expelling deep into her womb a hot river of ejaculation. Her neck muscles grew taut as she flung her head back, her mouth a tight line as she tried to keep herself from crying out. Climaxing, her torso heaving violently under him, a tiny but unmistakable cry escaped her.

Panting, her full breasts heaving, her eyes were smoky as she looked up at him. "You must come with me to Oregon," she told him.

"Oregon? With you?"

"Of course." She smiled and licked her lips wickedly. "We go so well together, don't you think?"

"We do, Kathleen, but Oregon is not where I am headed."

"Why not?"

"I have other plans."

She glared at him with smoldering resentment. Suddenly, she was like a summer storm—sunshine one moment, thunder and lightning the next. "I am not in the habit of being tossed aside so lightly," she informed him. "I made you an offer and you did not even appear to give it serious consideration."

He grinned at her. "All I said was that I had other plans. And I do."

"And just what are they?"

His smile faded. "I'm sorry, Kathleen. But isn't that my business? I'm sure you would make a man very happy. And Oregon sounds like a great place. But this here's my country and that's where I'm staying."

"I see," she said icily, her voice rising sharply. "You prefer this wilderness—the company of these untutored savages—to me!"

As gently as he could, he placed a large, powerful hand over her mouth. "Shh," he whispered. "You said we had to be quiet. The Widow Martin might hear us!"

She slapped his hand away. "Please," she bristled. "If you don't mind . . . !"

Hawk saw at once that the welcome mat was no longer in place. Reluctantly, he said, "I guess I'd better be getting back on guard, Kathleen. I'm sorry if I have angered you."

"I expected too much from you, Jed. Oregon is fine country, a place for a man and a woman to make a new beginning. I made a mistake, I guess."

"Maybe you ought to get to know Long Tom."

"He's a Harvard man," she sniffed. "They aren't very practical, but maybe he's an exception."

"I heard that, ma'am," Long Tom said, his head looming up in the wagon entrance, a big grin on his face. "And I take it kindly. You're right. I *am* an exception."

Kathleen blushed crimson and pulled a sheet up over her breasts. Chuckling, Hawk grabbed his britches and clambered past Long Tom, snatching up his rifle as he did so.

As Tom joined Hawk under the wagon a moment later, he looked over at Hawk and winked. "Some woman, that."

Hawk did not reply. She was some woman if you wanted to marry her and move to Oregon, but that was sure as hell not what he wanted.

— 3 —

The ground mists were glowing with the day's first light when a woman in the next wagon shrieked in terror.

Wide awake in an instant, Hawk scrambled out from under the widow's wagon and flung himself into the next one, bowie unsheathed. He had barely enough time to notice the settler crumpled against the tailgate, his scalped skull stove in, before he found himself wrestling with a Bannock. The Indian had been bent over the woman who had screamed, his breechclout dropped below his knees, one hand over the woman's mouth to prevent a second outcry.

Hampered by his lowered clout, the Bannock went down under Hawk's furious onslaught. Once, twice, Hawk plunged the blade of his bowie into the Indian's chest. Avoiding the spurting blood as best he could, he grabbed the inert Bannock by the hair, flung him out of the wagon, and struck another Bannock who was about to boost himself into the wagon.

Hawk flung himself at the second Bannock and caught him about the chest, bearing him to the ground. They hit with such force that the Indian remained where he had fallen while Hawk was flung forward over his head. As he scrambled to his feet, a third Bannock struck him from behind with his war club. The club did not catch him squarely, or it would have crushed his skull. It was enough to cause a brilliant explosion of light deep within his skull, however, and Hawk felt his knees turning to water as he sank to the ground. Glancing up, he saw the second Bannock push the other one aside and lift his own long knife to finish off Hawk.

Long Tom's rifle thundered from the widow's wagon, the ball catching the second Bannock in the face. When the other Bannock turned to face Tom, Hawk reached up and pulled him down, plunging his already bloody bowie into the Indian's belly, ripping the warrior open like a ripe melon.

It was now daylight. Glancing around, warm blood seeping down the back of his neck, Hawk saw the clearing inside the wagons alive with settlers and Bannocks locked in individual combat. The settlers, fighting for all they owned and loved, were putting up as ferocious and tenacious a fight as the Indians. Hawk saw a woman club a Bannock from behind with the blade of a shovel. The result was not pretty, but it sure as hell was effective. This spirited a defense soon proved to be too much for the feckless Bannocks. Looting this wagon train was proving too costly—much too costly.

Even as Hawk looked about him to ward off any more attackers, the Indians vanished beyond the wagons into the boulder field, carrying off with them their wounded and dead. As Hawk wiped off his blade on the dew-laden grass and straightened up, Long Tom hopped down from Hester Martin's wagon and hurried over to him.

"You all right, Hawk?"

"Thanks to you. That was a fine shot."

Long Tom grinned. "Well, I owed you one."

The two men glanced around. The canvas on one wagon was still smoldering. In the clearing huddled groups surrounded the wounded, while the dead were being wrapped in temporary shrouds by their women and children, many of whom cried openly. The sound of their broken sobs filled the encampment with an awful sense of desolation. Hawk was reminded of a similar scene of destruction many long years before in Texas while he and his sister looked on, their hearts heavy with loss and terror.

Angus MacLennan hurried over, his face grim with resolve.

"How many did you lose?" Hawk asked him.

"Two men and a woman who went to the aid of her husband. Three others have been wounded badly, John Barley especially. Those heathens used their war clubs to awful effect, I must admit."

"You'll find another dead settler in that wagon,"

Hawk informed him, pointing to the wagon where he had killed the Bannock. "And you better send someone to comfort his wife. What she was witness to wasn't very pretty."

Angus thanked Hawk and hurried off to see to it.

Burying their dead with a dispatch revealing a grim understanding of their situation, the settlers moved out by noon. The wagon train followed the stream that split the valley, and close to sundown they reached the end of the valley. There they camped and moved on the next morning without incident, Hester Martin's wagon in the lead with Kathleen MacLennan driving the oxen, the pale and subdued widow sitting beside her.

About midday Hawk saw a line of Blackfoot sitting on their ponies a mile or so away on a low ridge. He watched them warily, as did the rest of the settlers, until they vanished. That night Hawk and Long Tom told the settlers to post guards. They did so without complaint, but the night passed without any visit from the Indians.

For the third day in a row, Long Tom walked alongside Kathleen and the Widow Martin's wagon, and that night he joined Hawk on a log close by the fire. Hawk was sipping what passed for coffee and Long Tom took out his clay pipe and lit up, confessing to Hawk his keen desire for a mount. Only these fool settlers and digger Indians should have to walk over such uneven, treacherous ground.

"If you could leave off thinking of Kathleen for a night, we might be able to steal ourselves mounts from those Blackfoot we saw back there," Hawk replied, grinning sidelong at Long Tom.

"Man, that woman's something, ain't she?" Long Tom remarked with a grin, pipe smoke coiling upward about his face.

Hawk shrugged and said nothing.

"We talked for a while last night before she retired," Long Tom said, puffing contentedly on his pipe. "She's a real good-lookin' filly, and that's the truth. She seemed most interested in what I've been putting in my journals." He chuckled. "Seems to think I should go back to Harvard and teach."

"Maybe she's right. And maybe she's the woman for you. But I've heard tell the hardest stone in all creation is in a woman's breast."

"That's true enough, Hawk. I'd be the first to admit it. But it don't make sense for a man to be without a woman—nor for a woman to be without a man. It's a devilish arrangement, I admit, but there's no way a mortal can change that."

"What's all this about you being a Harvard man?"

"Well, now, it's like this, Hawk. Up in New England, most folks think that any man who goes to Harvard College or teaches there is hopelessly impractical, despite all his book-learning. They got a saying, 'You can always tell a Harvard man, but you can't tell him much.' "

"And you were a professor there?"

"That's the truth of it, hoss. I taught biology."

"Then what in blazes are you doing out here in this wilderness fighting with Blackfoot and grizzlies?"

"Hoss, can you imagine what a treasure these mountains are for a trained biologist? Back in my cabin I have a trunk of notebooks filled with observations and sketches of not only the flora of this region, but also much of its wildlife." For a moment he puffed on his pipe; then he went on, "When I return and publish these journals, hoss, I will astound all those armchair biologists back there and refute most of their hidebound theories. No, hoss, I'm not sorry for a single day I've spent out here. It's where I belong."

"You sure don't look like a professor—or a biologist."

Long Tom leaned back and laughed softly. "Hoss, that's been one of the blessings of this wilderness. Out here a man can let his manners and speech relax. He can let his hair grow—and let the wolf in him howl to the moon, if that's what he desires." He grinned at Hawk. "And a bath only when it suits him. You have no idea how pinched and mean are the manners and customs of that eastern world I left behind."

"I can imagine. But if you're going on to Oregon, what about that cabin of yours and them notes you took?"

"The cabin is well-hid. Only the grizzlies know of it, and they will tell no man. Never fear, I will return for those journals in good time."

"I take it you expect these fool pilgrims to take direction from you."

He took his pipe from his mouth and nodded. "Yes, I do, hoss, now that the Bannocks are off lickin' their wounds. John Barley's still half out of his head in his wagon; so he's no source of complaint, and Angus is already lookin' on me as a potential brother-in-law."

"Oregon's a long way from here, Tom."

"I know that, hoss. We'll just take it one step at a time. There's a fort up ahead beyond the next pass. Brett's Fort. I know it. It's an American Fur Company post. We'll stop there to lick our wounds, and Angus thinks it would be a good idea to wait there for the rest of their people to catch up to them."

"You mean there's more of these pilgrims on the way?"

"Yep. Another large wagon train, larger than this one. So it looks like we'll be holing up at Brett's Fort for a while before heading for South Pass."

"How long do you think it'll take before you move on?"

"That's hard to tell. Depends on when the rest of the pilgrims get there."

"Well, good luck to you, then." Hawk threw the dregs of his coffee into the fire. "I'll be pulling out first thing in the morning."

"Where you goin'?"

"To find that stream filled with beaver I was hunting when that first Blackfoot band found me." He peered closely at Long Tom. "You got any idea where I might find it?"

"I think I know just the one you're lookin' for, hoss."

"Where is it?"

"If I told you, it would be hid no longer. The rest of your beaver-hunting companions would soon have it cleaned of beaver, all for the sake of commerce in men's hats. Not on your life, Hawk."

"I would tell no one else. Why should I, Tom?"

"That's not the point. Why not let the beaver alone, Hawk? Leave this land as you find it."

"How do you know I won't do just that, Tom? All I want is a quiet stream to sit by—a place to rest up. All I know for sure is that the stream is high in these mountains somewhere and is surrounded by snow-capped peaks the year round. I can just imagine it, the air icy clear in the winter, alive with the sound of living things in summer. I won't trap the stream out, Tom. I'll take just enough beaver to keep me respectable at the next rendezvous."

"I wish I could believe you, hoss."

"Then you won't tell me?"

Long Tom took the pipe from his mouth and spat into the fire. "Hell, I don't need to. You'll find it yourself sooner or later."

"You could make it easy for me, Tom."

Long Tom thought awhile, then glanced sidelong at Hawk. "I'll tell you this much: you were headin' in the right direction when I first caught sight of you on horseback with them Blackfoot on your tail."

Hawk smiled. "Thanks."

They were silent for a while, the only sound the crackling fire at their feet. The pleasant fragrance of Long Tom's pipe filled the air about them. At last Hawk found himself unable to quell his curiosity, and he decided to go ahead and ask Long Tom a question that was not usually put to another man in this country.

"Tell me," he said, turning to Long Tom, "what's your real name? It sure ain't Long Tom, I know."

The corners of Long Tom's eyes crinkled as he chuckled. "Can you keep a secret?"

"Maybe."

"Algernon Percival Farrington . . ."

"My God!"

". . . the third."

"Your secret is safe with me, Tom."

The two men said nothing further about it. After a while, Long Tom finished his pipe and knocked the bowl's contents out on the side of the log. Then he bid Hawk good-night, got up, and strode over to the Widow Martin's wagon— and the waiting Kathleen MacLennan.

As Hawk watched him pull to a halt alongside her and doff his cap, he felt relief—not envy—at having escaped that fierce, dark-eyed woman's web.

Or did he?

The Blackfoot maiden was swimming across the pool with long, easy strokes, her dark hair trailing serpentlike behind her. Hawk moved down the slope, then stepped silently onto the broad back of a huge boulder sitting along the pool's rim. A birch clump hid him effectively; the Indian girl did not see him. He peered eagerly through the leaves at her, marveling at the smooth, sensuous rhythm of her strokes and her long, clean limbs.

She was at least eighteen, he judged, and was probably already married to some Blackfoot buck. But the sight of her frolicking in the water as gracefully and playfully as an otter had drawn him down from the ridge, and he could not take his eyes off her. He remembered Long Tom's words: "It don't make sense for a man to be without a woman." And watching this one, Hawk understood just what Long Tom meant. It had been a long, long time for him to be without a woman, and of late he had found himself thinking of Singing Wind—the lovely Crow woman he'd loved—without pain now, but with a steady, insistent longing.

Her swim finished, the girl stroked toward a small pile of deerskin clothing resting on a flat rock. Hawk watched her hungrily as she lifted, streaming, out of the water and approached the rock, her dark pubic patch dripping, her gleaming breasts firm, each nipple erect from the cold water. She did not dress at once, but faced the water and with a quick motion of her head flipped her long dark tresses down across her breasts. Then she parted them into two great flowing ribbons, combed each one out thoroughly, and then swiftly braided them.

Only when she turned back to reach for her buckskin dress did she catch sight of him through the birches. Uttering a tiny cry, she snatched up her dress and held it before her for an instant before ducking her head into it and shaking it down over her slim, damp body.

"Who are you?" she asked angrily, slipping on her moccasins.

In very poor Blackfoot, Hawk replied, "Do not be angry. I will not hurt you. I was passing and saw what I thought was a large otter swimming, and when I came closer, I saw it was you. To play so in the water will make the otters and the fish jealous."

"Your talk is silly. How are you called?"

He moved farther out onto the rock until he was completely visible to her. Going down on one knee, he leaned upon his rifle, which he planted, stock down, onto the boulder. "I am just a passing stranger."

"The Blackfoot tongue is not yours. Perhaps you should speak to me in Comanche, Golden Hawk."

He was only a little surprised that she should know his name. "Do you know Comanche, then?"

"Some."

"Speak in your own tongue."

"You will not understand me."

"What is there for me to understand?"

"That I am the woman of Beaver Tail."

"I am jealous of Beaver Tail. He must be a fine warrior indeed to have such a woman as you to tend his fire and comfort his bed."

She made a slight face to indicate her lack of enthusiasm for her husband's ability as a provider. "He has no pony herd, and when the other braves return to their lodges with buffalo and elk meat, he comes with rabbits and marmots. Still, he does not beat me and he is my husband, and he will have no other one see me as you just have."

"Then do not tell him."

She smiled then, a brilliant, devilish smile. "He already knows, Golden Hawk."

In that instant Hawk caught the flick of her glance at the slope behind him. Whirling, he saw Beaver Tail leap for him, knife in hand. Hawk ducked and flung up his hand to ward off the knife thrust. But Beaver Tail had misjudged the distance between them and, in his eagerness to take Hawk by surprise, missed him completely. The brave came down hard onto the boulder's surface, then tumbled backward and off the edge. The rear of his head struck the trunk of one of the birch trees and his skull broke open. An ugly red stain appeared on the white bark. Dropping his knife, the hapless Indian tumbled into the water and sank. From the point where he went under, a dark stain spread slowly.

It had all happened so quickly that Hawk felt nothing—only a kind of giddy amazement that he should escape the unexpected attack unscathed. He looked down at the woman standing on the bank.

"It is true what they say," she said, her voice hushed. "Golden Hawk has great magic. No warrior can stand before him. At night he becomes the Great Cannibal Owl and lives high in the pine trees. And to vanquish a foe, he has only to raise his hand. I have seen this."

"I did not mean to kill your husband."

"But you did."

"And now you are my responsibility."

"Yes, it is true. I am yours now. You are my master."

"No. I would be your husband instead."

"Golden Hawk speaks like a silly white man. A husband is always master, or he is no husband. But I do not worry. If Golden Hawk is my master now, he will not be so for long. Hear my words, Golden Hawk. I speak the truth."

Hawk dropped from the boulder and landed lightly beside her. "You may speak the truth, yet your words are riddles to me. Be clear, woman."

She tossed her head defiantly. "Wolf Heart has long wanted me. He is a great medicine man and war chief of my band. I have heard him speak of you to my father. Though your medicine is powerful, your heart is not strong, he says. You cannot look into a man's eyes and kill him slowly. This is what Wolf Heart tells my people."

"Do you believe him?"

"Yes. Wolf Heart has very powerful medicine. His father was Coyote Spirit, a great healer and conjurer of the wolf clan, one who could bring the thunder and lightning to a lodge, then send it back again. He taught Wolf Heart many great and fearsome things. He will take me from you someday."

"You think so, do you?"

She shrugged. "We will speak no more of it. What will happen will happen. Where is your lodge?"

"I have none."

"It is true, then. Golden Hawk sleeps in the pine tops."

"I am searching for a valley—one with a very rich beaver population. I was on my way there when I saw you."

Her eyes narrowed. "I know of such a valley."

"Take me to it, and there we will build our lodge."

"It is a long way from here."

"That does not matter. Take me there."

"You ask much of me—you who have done nothing to make me care for you. The corpse of my husband will float to the surface soon, his stomach bloated, his face as pale as the moon. Stones will bounce off his body as off a dead log floating in the water. Why should I take you where you want to go?"

He shrugged. "You said it yourself. I am your master."

"If you *are* my master, show me."

"Now?"

"Yes, now—unless the magic of the great Golden Hawk is no match for such a poor woman as me."

Her eyes had begun to glow—as if a fire raged behind them. Her taunting words, her whole manner, Hawk realized, had been meant to challenge and arouse him to action. She wanted to know what manner of man this Golden Hawk was, how much goading from a woman he could take. Now, this bold challenge of hers was a measure of her impatience, and of her desire for him to take her if he could.

Hawk grabbed her by the shoulders and drew her closer. Squirming quickly out of his grasp, she turned and ran up the embankment. He overtook her on a small grassy sward, grabbed her about the waist, and flung her to the ground. She kicked wildly, viciously up at him. He managed to grab both her ankles and, thrusting aside her legs, threw himself down upon her.

Her face dark with rage or passion—he could not be sure which—she twisted violently in an effort to dislodge him. When he attempted to kiss her, she tried to bite him. But he was patient, and it was not long before she realized the futility of trying to dislodge her new master. She grew still beneath him and allowed his lips to close about hers.

Their tongues entwined, Hawk peeled out of his buckskins and pulled up her dress. She flung it off and began to move under him restlessly, moaning softly. He fastened his lips about one of her nipples. It was as hard as a bullet, and as he pulled on it, she slipped her fingers into his heavy shock of hair to press his lips down harder upon her breast.

She sighed. "You have great medicine, Golden Hawk. But you cannot deny it. You are a man like any other."

He did not deny it. What was there to deny?

— 4 —

Her name was Running Moon, and for two days they camped by the pool, frolicking like otters, making love, getting used to each other. She boasted that she was the favored daughter of Elk Head, a famous war chief. Though she was as obedient as any good Blackfoot wife could be, Hawk could sense her holding a part of herself aloof from him. She did not try to excuse or deny this aloofness, but since it in no way impaired her willingness to lie with him or the skill and diligence with which she performed her camp chores, he ignored it. As far as Hawk was concerned, he had found for himself a willing bed mate and an efficient wife. If she was too proud to give in to him completely, that only made her the more desirable. Hawk understood and admired her reserve.

Meanwhile, they had only one horse.

Earlier, Hawk recalled, Running Moon had spoken with barely disguised scorn of Beaver Tail's performance as a provider, and when Hawk examined the quality of the couple's only mount—a stringy, loose-hipped pinto—he understood what she meant. Scornfully, in bitter Blackfoot phrases Hawk found less and less difficult to follow, she told of the shame she had felt as she walked rather than rode beside her husband whenever their band moved to new campsites. It was for this reason that, a few days before, Beaver Tail had left the White Lodge band and struck out on his own with Running Moon. The unspoken ridicule he saw every day in the eyes of the other band members was unbearable to him. Listening to Running Moon tell of this, Hawk realized just how expendable Beaver Tail had been all along.

Unwilling to chance a journey of any distance on such a sorry animal, Hawk decided to let Running Moon ride the horse, while he walked alongside, a shocking breach for an Indian couple, but one that Hawk was able to convince Running Moon to accept. He knew this only increased her scorn for his soft, white heart—but he expected this and gave it no heed.

In keeping with her promise, Running Moon headed northwest, in the direction she assured him would take them to that hidden valley where the beaver and otter filled the streams and pools that flowed through it. Barely a half-day's journey, however, was enough for the luckless pinto. He halted, swayed drunkenly, went down first on his hind legs, then his forelegs. As Running Moon jumped free, the pinto rolled over onto its side, lay its head down, and closed its eyes. It was not dead, but it was obviously not going to take Running Moon any farther.

Hawk yanked off the saddle, a clumsy contrivance of wood and canvas that barely deserved to be called such, and flung it into the woods. The horse uttered a kind of broken sigh at his deliverance, struggled to its feet, and ambled crookedly off into the timber.

Exasperation flared in Running Moon's dark, lovely eyes as she turned and looked up at Hawk. "Now we both walk to your valley where the stream is thick with beaver," she told him, "but it will be a long walk for both of us."

"No," Hawk replied, gazing after the vanished pinto. "I have been thinking on this since first I laid eyes on that poor beast. We need horses. Now we go to your people. The valley will come later."

"You will steal ponies from my people?"

"If I cannot purchase them. You say that your father is a famous chief and that you are his favorite daughter. I am sure he will welcome you and your new husband. From him I hope to purchase three fine ponies, one for each of us, and one for the beaver plews we will be packing to the next rendezvous."

"What do you have to buy such ponies?"

"In these saddlebags I carry many silver and gold coins. With these your father can purchase many fine items at any trading post—rifles, flour, sugar, rum."

Hawk had accummulated his wealth during

the past year by providing fresh venison for the inhabitants in and around Fort Hall. But his hope now was to live off what he could make as a trapper of beaver and otter, like so many other mountain men he had come to know. Besides, that part of him that would remain forever Indian had difficulty believing in the value of these coins, heavy and glittering though they might be. His hope was that Elk Head would see these coins as a white man would, as representing the power to purchase much that was valuable to them.

"We will see," Running Moon said. "But I think my father would rather have a fine buffalo coat or a new rifle. That one of yours would bring many fine ponies, I think."

"That is not for sale. It belonged to my father. I took it from the Comanche chief who killed him."

She shrugged her shoulders and turned her head to face north. "Then we will go to my people. If that is what you wish. But I think you are a fool, husband. My people know of you and fear you like frightened children fear the shadows of the dead. And in my village is one who hates you, Wolf Heart."

"It does not matter. All I want is to purchase horses—or steal them, if it comes to that. It will not be unjust if I steal them. It is because of a Blackfoot war party that I lost a fine stud black."

She did not deign to comment as she started off through the timber ahead of him, walking with swift, sure steps back toward her people's village.

After a three days' journey they came to Running Moon's village. It was in a valley just east of the Little Rockies. The valley's most notable landmark was a high butte that Running Moon called French Cap. A good name for it, Hawk noted, since the top of the butte was covered with a dense growth of pine, giving it the appearance of a ragged wool cap worn by some French trappers. The Blackfoot lodges were spread out over the length of a fine grassy glade, following the course of a broad mountain stream that meandered the length of the valley. Hawk glimpsed the horse herds farther up the stream. There were many fine head, enough to fill several large, birch-bordered meadows.

In full view, they walked boldly toward the village, Running Moon keeping a dutiful three or four steps behind him. She was packing not only her own gear but his saddlebags as well. Hawk was well-armed: his bowie knife was in its case and his Hawkins, loaded and primed, was slung on a rawhide thong across his back. His throwing knife remained invisible in its sheath at the back of his neck, and his braided rawhide reata, looped closely, hung on his belt. Though he was ready for trouble, he hoped it would not come; he was counting on Wolf Heart to remember his debt to Hawk and intercede if things got too hot. And if Wolf Heart did not help him, Hawk would simply have to count on the fact that he was now the husband of Elk Head's daughter.

Hawk made no effort to keep his identity a secret from the Blackfoot. His long yellow hair had been combed out and rested neatly on his powerful shoulders. He wore his fringed buckskin shirt and his finest fringed buckskin trousers, with their bright, beaded vinework running along the outer seams. On his feet he wore a pair of moccasins with stiff rawhide soles and soft buckskin uppers; he had suffered long and hard with white man's boots before giving them away to a settler in Fort Hall and reverting to the footgear he had known for so long as a Comanche.

Long before they reached the village, their approach had been reported. Now, as they neared the first lodge, Hawk noted how profoundly silent the village was. No dogs barked, and even the children were quiet. A mounted warrior appeared from behind one of the lodges and rode out to block their path, his lance pointed at Hawk's heart.

Beside him, a nervous Running Moon whispered, "Be careful. This brave is of the Crazy Dog band."

"Do you see your father's lodge?"

"It is many lodges away on a small hillock near the stream. I see it, but I do not see my father."

"You are Golden Hawk," said the mounted warrior.

Hawk shrugged. "I do not deny this," he replied, his Blackfoot clumsy but serviceable.

"You have many enemies in these lodges," the Crazy Dog soldier replied. "Old men and widows still weep and grieve because of you. But Chief Elk Head has forbidden me to kill you. He fears your medicine."

"He has nothing to fear. Neither do you or any of your people. I come in peace with Running Moon. She is now my woman. And I am proud to be her husband."

"I tell you this for the last time," the brave told Hawk, steadying his lance. "You may keep your scalp only if you and your woman leave this village."

"Is this the famous Blackfoot hospitality?"

"I have told you. You are not welcome in this village."

Running Moon squared her shoulders and spoke out angrily. "Hear my husband! Do as he says! His medicine is powerful! I have seen this. He can bring this village good luck or bad. Which do you choose?"

The mounted Blackfoot's face paled at the threat, but he was not a coward. Pulling up his lance, he snatched up his bow and, fitting his arrow's notch to the string, drew it back, the arrowhead aimed directly at Hawk's heart. It would be but a second for the Crazy Dog soldier to send the shaft into Hawk's heart. And from the look of pure resolve on the warrior's face, Hawk realized his time had come.

Running Moon gasped in horror.

A sharp command halted the soldier. Slowly, the mounted warrior lowered his bow. Hawk glanced over to see a familiar figure striding out of his lodge. Wolf Heart. He walked past the Crazy Dog soldier and came to a halt in front of Hawk. The mounted Blackfoot returned his arrow to its quiver. Behind Wolf Heart, Hawk noticed, the Blackfoot men and women stole silently from their lodges to watch. Hawk was not surprised to recognize among them three of the Blackfoot warriors who had trapped him on the cliff high above the falls.

"I welcome you, Golden Hawk," Wolf Heart said. "You may stay in my lodge as my guest."

"Many thanks, Wolf Heart."

The Crazy Dog warrior nudged his pony aside to let them pass. At once the villagers became active spectators and pushed closer to see Golden Hawk and Running Moon. Somewhere in the camp a dog barked, and the sharp cries of children could be heard. A rising murmur of voices came from the spectators crowding closer. The great warrior and magician Wolf Heart had offered his hospitality to the legendary Golden Hawk. Now they would see what would come of this meeting.

Wolf Heart led them to his lodge. It bore upon its north and south side a huge black-and-red pictograph of a wolf, symbol of the Timber Wolf, indicating that Wolf Heart was a firm believer in the faith of his father's tribe, the Timber Wolf clan and a believer in his father's magic as well.

Wolf Heart flipped aside the flap to his lodge and ducked through the hole, Hawk and Running Moon following in after him. Several women, one of them very old, sat huddled together near the entrance. Wolf Heart sat upon his couch and with an abrupt motion of his hand indicated that Hawk should take a seat to his left. Running Moon took her place with the women, crouching down beside them.

Above Wolf Heart's seat, securely tied to the lodgepoles, hung his medicine pipe, bound in otter and sable skins. Spread over his backrest at the right end of his couch was the skin of a mountain lion. In front of him rested his everyday pipe of black stone resting upon a large flat stone, his tobacco in a pouch beside it.

As he filled the pipe with a mixture of American Fur Company tobacco and a sweet herb, Hawk hoped he would use plenty of the herb, since he knew the American Fur Company's tobacco to be quite strong. Wolf Heart passed the pipe to Hawk to light, after which the two men smoked the pipe in turns. At last the pipe was put aside, and one of Wolf Heart's wives set before them the well-boiled brains of some small animal. During the meal Wolf Heart—though he did not look at her directly—observed Running Moon closely. Hawk had no doubt that Running Moon was observing Wolf Heart just as eagerly.

Hawk was bemused. He had come to this village to purchase three mounts from Running Moon's father and had almost been struck down upon entering the village. He would be dead now if it were not for Wolf Heart's intercession. As Hawk had hoped, the Blackfoot Indian remembered his debt and paid it. Now the two men were even, except for the fact that, as twisted fate would have it, Hawk had shown up with the woman Wolf Heart wanted.

"My heart is glad to see Wolf Heart again," Hawk said as the women took away the food bowls.

Wolf Heart smiled. As before, it was the warrior's eyes that riveted Hawk. They were like the unblinking orbs of a large, feral animal. A bear, perhaps—or a wolf.

"Wolf Heart is glad also," the Indian said, leaning forward slightly, his voice sibilant. "Now that his offer of hospitality has saved Golden Hawk's life, he no longer owes him a life. This warrior is free now to hang Golden Hawk's yellow hair on his scalp pole. Then will Golden Hawk's medicine join with that of Wolf Heart. He will become the most famous medicine man of all the Blackfoot lodges."

Hawk shrugged. "Take my scalp when you can, Wolf Heart. You may find that difficult. But for now, I am your guest and this conversation bores me. I came to Running Moon's village to purchase three ponies. I will pay for them in white man's gold. I had hoped to speak to Running Moon's father, since he has such a fine herd. But you will do instead, if it is your wish."

"This Blackfoot warrior has no wish for the white man's gold or for his silver. He will send for Elk Head." Wolf Heart glanced over at a small boy huddled next to his mother near the entrance. The medicine man's iron glance was enough to send the boy from the lodge in an instant.

Wolf Heart smiled at Hawk. "Golden Hawk speaks the truth. Not only has this chief a large herd of many fine ponies, he has sired a strong-willed daughter, one suitable for a man with such powerful medicine as Golden Hawk—or this

Blackfoot warrior." As he spoke, he looked boldly past Hawk at Running Moon—an insolent afront to Hawk, and meant to be just that.

Hawk smiled coolly. "Keep your eyes to yourself, Wolf Heart. Running Moon is my woman now. Wolf Heart has many women to tend his hearth fire. He does not need more. And the daughter of Elk Head would not shame her father by leaving me now to live with you—unless I am dead, of course."

Wolf Heart nodded darkly. "Yes. Unless the great Golden Hawk is dead."

Elk Head entered the lodge then, proudly but deferentially, without a glance at his daughter. Wolf Heart indicated with a wave of his hand that the old chief should sit beside him on the couch. Elk Head's long robes swayed as he strode across the lodge's interior to sit beside Wolf Heart. Hawk could hear the fringes scraping lightly against the doeskin surfaces and also the delicate chink of tiny bells sewn into his seams. An important chief of the Blackfoot, Elk Head wore what appeared to be his finest eagle-feather war bonnet, one laden with ermine tails, ermine skins, and shiny brass tacks. Evidently the chief had been expecting Wolf Heart's summons and had dressed accordingly.

Still not glancing at his daughter, Elk Head fixed his powerful black eyes on Golden Hawk. In them Hawk recognized the same spirited arrogance that animated Running Moon. Indeed, everything about this chief impressed him, from his craggy brow to the square set of his jaws and the wide, expressive line of his mouth. He was a truly handsome Blackfoot.

"Golden Hawk is very brave and also very foolish to come to this Blackfoot village with the stolen daughter of a famed war chief," Elk Head reminded Hawk in Blackfoot. "He does not fear the wrath of the many Blackfoot who have burned their lodges and lopped off their fingers because of his skill in battle, his fierce and terrible deeds." He shook his head in wonder. "Truly, his medicine is powerful."

Hawk accepted this with a slight, barely perceptible nod.

"What is it that Golden Hawk wishes from a chief of the White Lodge Blackfoot?"

"Horses."

"How many?"

"Three."

His eyes on Hawk's rifle, Elk Head asked almost eagerly, "And what does the mighty Golden Hawk offer in return?"

Taking out his leather pouch, Golden Hawk spilled onto the robe in front of the chief ten silver dollars and two twenty-dollar gold pieces. For an instant Elk Head's expression revealed the disappointment he felt at not being offered something more tangible and immediately useful, such as Hawk's rifle. But as he studied the pile of coins before him, his eyes gleamed in satisfaction. Evidently, he understood fully the uses of such coins, and knew he could purchase much of value with them at the Fort Hall trading post later that summer.

The chief nodded his acceptance and said, "Elk Head does not bargain with Golden Hawk. And he does not wish many fine gifts in exchange for his daughter—only his promise that he will not beat her and that he will see to it that she does not again have to walk while he rides."

"Agreed."

Gathering up the coins, the chief got to his feet. Speaking loudly so that all in the lodge would hear him, he said, "This chief will look now upon the face of his daughter. Since her departure with the wretched Beaver Tail, his heart has sat like a stone in his breast. His heart is light now and soars with the eagle, for she has returned to his village as the woman of Golden Hawk. For too long has his lodge been empty of her laughter."

The chief strode past Hawk and paused before Running Moon. She gazed up at her father with great affection, then sprang into his arms, hugging him with great warmth. A moment later the two left Wolf Heart's lodge together, Hawk following.

— 5 —

Hawk and Elk Head were in one of the farthest meadows, selecting the three ponies they had bargained for when two high-sided, horse-drawn wagons appeared in the northern flanks of the valley, heading for the Blood village. The trade wagons were escorted by well-armed mounted outriders. One of the wagons displayed a small Hudson's Bay Company flag.

By the time Elk Head and Hawk returned to the village, the men from the Hudson's Bay Company had halted their wagons in a small clearing close by the stream and were trading with the Indians. Hawk counted at least ten heavily armed men standing about the wagons, and realized there were probably more inside the wagons. Some Indians who had gone to the wagons to trade were returning empty-handed, Hawk noticed. It appeared that these well-armed traders from the Hudson's Bay Company were not all that interested in trading with the Indians and had stopped here for another purpose.

When Hawk and Elk Head drew closer to the village, two men left the wagons and hurried over to intercept them. One was a small, wiry fellow, as tough as burnished oak. He was a mountain man, judging from his greasy buckskins and the keen light in his small sharp eyes. His companion was an overdressed gentleman wearing a beaver felt hat, frock coat, white cotton shirt complete with a celluloid collar and string tie, dark trousers, and shiny black boots. His soft belly strained the buttons on his vest, and while his smaller, more fit companion moved as lightly as a deer, he swaggered.

Halting in front of Hawk and Elk Head, the overdressed gentleman from the Hudson's Bay Company ignored Elk Head and doffed his cap to Hawk.

"A white man! Good! I assume you speak English."

"I do," Hawk replied, mildly astonished at the man's foolish breach of manners. A guest in Chief Elk Head's village, he should have addressed Elk Head first, granting the chief the courtesy of a slight bow or nod of the head, at least.

"I am Thomas Empson. And who might you be?"

"I am Jed Thompson. And this here is Chief Elk Head."

"Yes, I was told that's who he was. Indeed, I have come a long way to see him. I assume you understand his wretched tongue. My scout here does not."

"Your scout? You haven't introduced us."

"Oh, of course. Pardon me. His name is Joe Meek."

Hawk directed a slight smile at the mountain man, who winked back at him. Joe Meek was perfectly well aware of the churlish qualities of this fathead from the Hudson's Bay Company.

"Now, then, Mr. Thompson, can we get on with it?" Empson demanded impatiently. "I want you to interpret for me. I really must speak with the chief."

"I warn you, I speak Blackfoot very poorly."

Empson waved away a cloud of small black flies with a handkerchief, from which wafted an overly sweet scent. "Poorly or not," Empson replied, "it will have to suffice. I will pay you well."

Ignoring the man's careless arrogance—and aware that Meek probably understood and spoke the Blackfoot tongue eloquently—Hawk smiled slightly and told him that he would do the best he could.

"Fine," Empson said, pleased. "Now, be so kind as to tell this lice-infested barbarian that I am very pleased to meet him."

Elk Head, who knew enough English to understand Empson, was not insulted by his words or manner. He understood perfectly that the man knew no better. His eyes gleaming at the mild deception, the chief waited for Hawk's translation of Empson's words before nodding a solemn, dignified greeting to Empson. The chief then asked Hawk to ask Empson why he had come so far to visit the White Lodge clan of the Blood Blackfoot.

Pleased at the directness of the question, Empson responded promptly. "It is our wish to forge an alliance between the Blackfoot people and the men of the Hudson's Bay Company."

Hawk relayed this to Elk Head. Through Hawk, the chief asked Empson the nature and purpose of this alliance.

Empson explained eagerly, "It as an alliance that will throw the American Fur Company out of these mountains."

"Throw them out?" Hawk asked Empson directly.

"Yes. They are outlaws, interlopers. Worse, they are stealing our beaver, setting up their illegal forts everywhere."

"Let me get this straight," said Hawk, no longer bothering to translate for Elk Head. "You want Chief Elk Head and his warriors to help you drive out the American Fur Company?"

"Precisely."

Hawk turned to face the chief to translate Empson's words, but Elk Head stopped him with an impatient wave of his hand. The chief understood as well as Hawk what Empson wanted, and this was no longer time for games. "You tell again what you want Blackfoot to do," he demanded of Empson.

Empson was a little taken aback to learn that the chief could speak English, after all. "Ah! Then you *do* speak English, Chief. Well, then! That makes things much simpler. Let me put it this way. I have men who are waiting to join your Blackfoot warriors in an attack on the forts belonging to the American Fur Company."

"Why?"

"I have already explained that. They are trapping illegally. These mountains belong to the Hudson's Bay Company."

"You are wrong. These mountains belong to everybody."

"Yes, yes—of course. But I don't mean the mountains. What I meant, Chief, was that for hunting and trapping the beaver and the otter and all the other fur-bearing animals, this is Hudson's Bay country. For that reason we are legally entitled to drive out the American Fur Company."

"Why you drive them off? They do same as you. They trade for beaver and other furs."

"But don't you see, Chief," Empson said in some exasperation. "That's just it. The beaver on this land does not belong to them."

"You are crazy, I think. The beaver belong to him who catch him."

"We have treaties and grants that prove the Hudson's Bay Company has first rights to trapping in these mountains. All we want now is your people's help in driving out these Americans."

"By driving out," Hawk said, "you mean attacking the forts, burning them and their goods."

Empson looked at Hawk. "Well, that is putting it plainly enough, and I do not deny it. I am afraid the company has no other recourse. It has been driven to it. I do not care about the American Fur Company's goods, however. The Blackfoot may keep them, if they wish. As fair booty."

The chief had been listening carefully. "You want us join you on war path against white skins? Take scalps? Kill?"

"Well, now, Chief, it shouldn't be necessary to go that far," Empson replied cautiously. "Scalping is a most unsightly practice and I had hoped we could forgo such barbarous practices. All that is required is that we drive out the fur traders. A few shots may be fired, of course, even a few killed—but only a few. Surely you can restrain your own warriors."

The chief looked at Hawk. "Restrain? What does he mean?"

"He wants you to hold your warriors back while they are fighting the traders and the mountain men so they will not kill too many."

"I cannot tell my braves how many scalps to take," Elk Head said, addressing Empson. "They not listen to me if I do, and then I will be no chief."

Through all this, though he was astounded and furious, Hawk kept his composure. The Hudson's Bay Company wanted the Blackfoot to join their men in driving the American Fur Company out of the mountains. He looked at Joe Meek. The man did not wink at him this time, but it was plain that Meek would be no party to any uprising with the Indians against the American Fur Company.

Elk Head turned to Hawk. In Blackfoot, he

said, "I do not think this man is a good man. Why he want Blackfoot to kill white faces? The beaver do not belong to his company. They belong to everybody. There is plenty beaver. I think he crazy. Tell him to go from here and take his wagons. The White Lodge band of Blackfoot will not join such a crazy man."

Relieved, Hawk turned to Empson. "The chief says no. He thinks you are crazy, Empson. He wants you and your wagons to get the hell out of this valley, and I suggest you do it."

Empson's face went scarlet. He turned to Joe Meek, as if to gain some support from the little mountain man. But Joe Meek was grinning up at him instead.

"That's what the chief said, Tom. I think maybe you better do what he says."

"I thought you couldn't understand Blackfoot tongue."

"I can now."

"You're fired as scout."

"You can't fire me. I already quit!"

In a fury, Empson whirled about and marched back to his wagons, Joe Meek making no effort to keep up with him.

That same day Hawk and Running Moon left the village astride their new ponies. Running Moon's three sisters and her one brother, in addition to her many friends and relatives, threw off their uneasiness caused by Hawk's presence and came to Elk Head's lodge to bid them good-bye. All of them brought presents. As a result, when Hawk and Running Moon started out, the pack horse was almost staggering under the load of furs and blankets, and the poles and skin of a small but serviceable tepee donated by Elk Head. Though Hawk planned to build a cabin before snowfall, he was quick to admit to Running Moon that until then, a tepee—even of modest size— would serve nicely.

Running Moon's departure from her father was correct and dignified, without an unseemly display of emotion, but this did not prevent Hawk from becoming aware of the deep emotion felt by each of them, made all the more touching by the iron discipline that allowed only one tear to move down Elk Head's cheek.

Looking back only once before they reached the timber, Running Moon waved to her robed father and the rest of his family, then nudged her pony resolutely to the northwest and urged it to a lope, Hawk following. Just before he reached the timber, Hawk glanced back at the village.

The Hudson's Bay Company's wagons had left the stream and were moving back the way they had come. Thomas Empson and his men had been sent packing by the Blackfoot and were lucky they still had their scalps after making such a preposterous proposition to them.

Frowning, Hawk saw more than a few Blackfoot trailing back from the spot where the wagons had halted. In their hands were brown whiskey jugs. If they contained the usual Hudson's Bay Company formula, it was a potent mixture indeed. This night would be filled with wild dancing, outcries, and deadly quarrels. Men would swap unwilling wives. Others would take wives they had lusted after. There would be knifings, and the sound of puking Indians would fill the air.

Hawk shuddered.

Turning back around in his saddle he entered the timber, Running Moon at his side.

The next day, about midafternoon, Hawk first noticed the large gray timber wolf on a ridge above their trail. He was obviously a male and was trotting parallel to them in that swift, half-loping gait typical of the wolf. Hawk paid little attention to him. Wolves traveled in packs, and few lone wolves had ever been known to attack men—and certainly not when two of them were mounted.

The wolf vanished soon thereafter and Hawk gave it no further thought. Close to twilight, he and Running Moon were entering a small glade beside a stream when from a slight hillock close by the trail, a heavy pale blur struck him like a thunderbolt. Hawk went flying off his horse and landed on his back, the fierce, maddened snout of a timber wolf ripping and tearing at his left forearm as Hawk flung it up instinctively to protect his face. On a slight incline, they rolled down it, Hawk still wrapped about the wolf's long body. When they came to a halt, Hawk reached back with his free right hand and grabbed his throwing knife. Repeatedly he plunged it into

the great fur muff about the wolf's neck, striking
the backbone once, slipping deep into soft flesh
another time.

But the maddened wolf would not pull back
and was close to shredding Hawk's arm, its hot
breath scalding Hawk's face, when Running Moon
appeared over them with Hawk's rifle and began
slamming the beast about its head and shoulders
with the heavy barrel. Uttering a series of high,
yelping cries, the wolf pulled back, turned, and
snapping once up at Running Moon, loped off.

On his back, Hawk cried, "The rifle's primed!
Shoot him!"

Running Moon ran up onto a bank to get a
clearer shot at the fleeing wolf, raised the rifle to
her shoulder, and fired. She watched a moment,
then sank, terrified, to the ground. On his feet in
an instant, Hawk ran up to her. Ignoring the pain
in his forearm, he took the rifle from her and
peered into the dim timber. He could not see the
wolf.

"Do you think you hit him?"

"No," she said, turning her face up to his,
tears coursing down her cheeks. "I do not think
so."

"Well, if the bastard shows up again, I'll put a
round through his black heart. That's a promise."

He saw a deep, terrible fear in her eyes. "No,"
she said fearfully. "I do not think you will,
husband."

"You don't? Just watch me."

She put her arms around him and hugged him
close. She was still shaking from the encounter.

He lifted her head to kiss away her tears. "You saved my life, Running Moon. My knife wasn't doing much good."

She did not respond at first, only hugged him all the closer. He responded, doing his best to comfort her—and not a little surprised at the extent of her concern for him.

"I am ashamed, husband," she told him softly, fearfully. "Before, I say to you that I want Wolf Heart to take me into his lodge and be his woman. But I do not want this anymore. It is only you I want."

"That is nice to hear, Running Moon."

She pulled away slightly and gazed up into his eyes. "So now I tell you secret. I lead you to this place you seek, only I take long way. But tomorrow we go short way, through narrow canyon. I think maybe we will be there by nightfall."

Hawk realized he should have chastised Running Moon for her deception. Instead, he only chuckled and hugged her to him. It was clear to him that, from now on, there would be no holding back with her. She was his completely.

Somewhere deep in the timber, a wolf lifted its head and sent a long, yelping howl into the sky. As the mournful cry faded, Running Moon buried her face in Hawk's chest and hugged him still closer.

— 6 —

Hawk was not disappointed. The beaver population in the valley was far more numerous than he could have imagined, the hollow slap of their tails echoing almost constantly. So plentiful was the game in the timbered slopes above their camp that the first thing Hawk did was to go tramping about with Running Moon to take a census of the animal population. Black bears and grizzlies were numerous, most of them preferring the high meadows and only occasionally venturing down to the stream. The black bears ran upon sight of them; the grizzlies did not run, but they kept their distance, since on each occasion Running Moon and Hawk sighted them, the bears were downwind of them and got a good, troubling whiff of their human scent.

A small herd of buffalo were bunched in the southern reaches of the valley, its members keeping to the fertile lowlands and splashing about in the reed-filled shallows. Wolverines also resided in the valley, their harsh squeal heard only at night. This gave Hawk pause when he considered how they might hinder his trapping. Once or twice Hawk heard the cry of a cougar from somewhere above him in the snowy fastness of the peaks that rimmed the valley, but neither he nor Running Moon ever caught sight of it. Rabbits, marmots, porcupines, and badgers abounded, the ground hog the most numerous of all. Hawk and Running Moon watched one tribe of them one day as they came and went among the rocks near the stream, feeding upon the grasses and tubers.

From the first, antelope and black-tailed deer nervously peered down at them from the edge of the timber, and only after a few days did they feel safe enough to leave their cover and move across the meadow below the tepee to drink at the stream and feed on the lush grass along its banks. Soon thereafter elk joined them, the racks on some of the bucks truly amazing.

On the fourth day after their arrival in the valley, Hawk and Running Moon were outside their lodge, enjoying the late-afternoon sunlight flooding the valley. Hanging over an outside fire, a venison stew was sending a mouth-watering aroma into the air. Into the simmering pot, Running Moon was stirring wild onions and tubers, pepper grass, and other herbs she had found along the riverbank. Not too far away, sitting cross-legged with his back to a tree, Hawk was

sharpening his bowie on a flat piece of sandstone
he had found the day before.

"Hawk!"

Hawk looked up to see a large grizzly approaching them, obviously drawn by the powerful smell
of the stew bubbling in the pot and the racks of
freshly jerked venison drying in the sun. The
grizzly was a big fellow, its hump gray with age.
It moved with a hesitant shambling gait down
the slope toward their lodge, pausing constantly
and lifting onto its hind legs to sniff the air, after
which it shambled eagerly closer. When it showed
no intention of shying away, Hawk got to his
feet.

"Go way, bruin," he shouted.

The bear hesitated.

Hawk waved his arms and took a couple of
steps closer to it. The bear appeared on the verge
of running, but it could smell the stew now—and
it must have been churning his stomach with
anticipation. Hawk grabbed up a frying pan and
his pistol and began banging on the frying pan
with the gun barrel. It was enough. Uttering a
disappointed *whoof*, the grizzly turned tail and
ambled hastily back toward the timber. But before it vanished into it, it glanced back at them,
and in that glance Hawk read not only disappointment, but a surly, brutish anger as well.

"I'll have to kill it," Hawk told Running Moon
regretfully, speaking to her now in a Blackfoot
that was almost fluent.

"It is very big."

"And it is old, but that does not matter much

with a grizzly. They die hard at any age." He put down the frying pan and stuck his pistol back into his belt.

"Maybe it will stay away now."

"I doubt it. Its nose tells it there is food here. Good food, too. Maybe, Running Moon, you should not be such a fine cook. Mr. Grizzly will be back. I will keep the rifle loaded and my powder horn and balls always near me."

She nodded and continued to stir the venison stew.

"The smell of that stew as much as the dry meat is what is drawing it," Hawk said. "From now on it would be better for us to eat only dried meat and coffee."

"Yes, husband. That is a fine idea. No more stew or wild carrots. Only dried meat and coffee. Then you will spend all your time squatting over the hole, and what will come out, no matter how much you grunt, will be little bullets. Then the grizzly will visit us again, only this time to see why you make such noise."

It was a grotesque scene her words conjured, and he laughed. "All right," he told her. "All right. We will continue to eat the stew. And tomorrow I will set out after the old grizzly."

Hawk saw the sudden apprehension in Running Moon's eyes. But she said nothing as she continued to stir the stew. Hawk went back to his place under the tree and resumed honing his knife.

Finding and tracking the grizzly was not difficult. In a clearing above the timber Hawk came upon it digging into a soft bank for tubers. When it saw Hawk, it sat up on its haunches and wiggled its nose as it sniffed the air. Hawk dismounted and walked closer. The grizzly left off its digging and charged down the slope. Hawk aimed carefully and fired. With a roar the grizzly rolled over, biting and clawing at its flank where the round had entered. Then it regained its feet and charged down the slope toward Hawk.

Hawk reloaded and fired. This time his round landed in the grizzly's hump, the force of the bullet turning the beast around. Pouring powder into his barrel, Hawk spat a ball into it, flung it up, and fired, this time shattering the bear's backbone. The bear began thrashing helplessly. Hawk ran up alongside the sprawled beast and finished him off with a deliberately aimed bullet in the base of the brain.

Inspecting the grizzly, Hawk was pleased. Despite its age, the grizzly had a fine coat of fur. It would make a perfect robe to throw over his bed while snug in his cabin on cold winter nights, the fire roaring in the fireplace—and Running Moon beside him under it, her long, naked loins thrust against his.

He set to work skinning the bear and found it no small task. It was quite fat, and Hawk had to work very hard to scrape the hide as clean as possible. Not until dusk did he ride up to his lodge, the bearskin flung over the pony's neck. Running Moon was in the tepee. He could see the hearth fire's smoke curling out of the flap and could smell the ribs and soup she was preparing. Quite pleased with himself, he leaned back in his saddle and called out to her.

She lifted the flap and stepped out, ready to welcome him.

"I found the old devil," Hawk commented, slipping off the horse and slapping the skin proudly. "Its skin will make a fine blanket for us this winter."

By this time she had drawn close enough to see what it was he had flung over the pony's neck. "*Kyai-yo*," she exclaimed, throwing up her hands in terror. Then, inexplicably, she flung about and ran back inside the tepee as if she had just seen the devil himself.

With a shrug, Hawk dumped the bearskin on the ground, then unsaddled his mount and led him over to graze alongside the other ponies. He was perplexed. Whenever he had returned from a hunt in the past, Running Moon inspected his kill eagerly, showing great pride in his skill, and would then insist upon unsaddling his mount and leading him away, asking questions all the while. Hawk had no idea what was wrong now, but he had long since learned to ignore the strange and mystifying moods of women.

Inside the lodge, Running Moon was waiting to serve him. She set down before him a plate of boiled boss ribs and a bowl of soup. As Hawk ate, he told Running Moon of the grizzly and how many rounds it had taken to stop it. She listened intently, but made no comment.

"It is a fine hide," Hawk concluded, "with

long thick, hair, very dark in spots. I wish you would tan it for me."

"No," she said firmly.

"But why not?"

She sighed. "Have pity on me, husband. I cannot touch the bearskin. Only here and there is a woman, or even a man, whose medicine is powerful enough to protect them while handling a bear skin."

"Protect them?"

"I have seen it. Always some great misfortune befalls any woman foolish enough to tan a bear's skin. Sickness, even death, follows. I tell you I have seen it. There is a woman of the Buffalo Chip band who would do it for you, but she is far from here."

"Well, then. I'll do it myself," Hawk said, laughing.

The next day, without much enthusiasm, Hawk set about tanning the bearskin. He stretched it by pegging it to the ground near the lodge and began scraping the skin off the hide with a flesher. Running Moon watched uneasily from the lodge entrance, and even when she went down to the stream to wash some clothing, she came back repeatedly to peer at him nervously, always from a safe distance.

Scraping off the skin was tedious work, and Hawk would have preferred working on the cabin he had started a few days before on the flat below the lodge. Throughout the day he kept at it, however, allowing himself only a few brief respites, during which he smoked the pipe Elk

Head had given him. By nightfall, his arms and torso covered with bear grease, he was pretty damn tired of the task and came wearily in to supper, grateful for the respite and aware that he was not doing a very good job of cleaning the bearskin.

The next morning he awoke soon after daylight. He could hear Running Moon praying near the lodge, telling her gods that she was about to take the bearskin flesh and tan it. She begged them to have mercy on her; she did not want to tan the bearskin; she feared to touch the unclean thing—but her man wished it to be worked into a soft robe.

"Oh, Sun," she concluded, "protect me from the evil power of the shadow of this bear. Let my good health continue. Give myself and my man a long life, happiness. Let us live to be old!"

Hawk pulled on his buckskins and hurried from the lodge. Running Moon was on her knees in the grass. Hurrying over to her, he went down on one knee beside her.

Putting his arms around her shoulders, he hugged her close. "Forget the bearskin," he told her. "It is not worth all this."

She pushed him away gently but firmly, shook her long black hair back off her shoulders, and got to her feet. He stood up also.

"It is enough that you want it, husband," she told him firmly. "You should not labor like a woman. If I allow such a thing, the gods will truly punish me. I will tan the bearskin for you and in the winter it will keep us warm."

She spoke bravely, but he felt the tremor in her voice and knew the terror in her heart. But this was what she wanted, and he told himself that when she tanned the bearskin and they used it, winter after winter, she would realize then that the shadows of dead animals had no power over the living. With that knowledge, one more fearsome superstition would be lifted from her soul.

"Thank you, Running Moon," Hawk said. "It will be the finest robe any man ever threw over his bed. You will see. It will bring us good fortune, for the spirit of this bear was brave indeed—just as you are."

It was a somber breakfast they had together and Hawk went down to the flat to resume work on the cabin, while above him, kneeling on the ground in front of it, Running Moon scraped steadily away at the bearskin, diligently continuing the work he had begun so poorly the day before.

At the end of five days the bearskin robe was finished and under it that night they huddled. Detecting Running Moon's nervousness, he attempted to console her, to explain that, in reality, the world was not populated with the ghosts of the dead, that so many of her terrors and those of her Blackfoot friends and relatives were groundless.

"What is this you say, husband?" she asked, perplexed, sitting up in their bed, her dark tresses coiling over her breasts. "Can you not transform yourself into the Great Cannibal Owl? At night, do you not fly from tree to tree like the hawk? Many of the Blackfoot tell of this around their fires. Some of our people in the north say they have witnessed your magic."

Patiently, Hawk explained his need to take his sister, Annabelle, back from the Blackfoot who had stolen her, and how this great need had forced him to use every means, even to convincing them that he was the Great Cannibal Owl.

"Then at night you do not become the Cannibal Owl?"

He laughed. "Are you disappointed?"

"It was a trick?"

"Yes."

"But you were seen!"

"My wings were branches cut from the pine, and the night made everything seem possible. I am a trickster—like Wolf Heart or any other conjurer."

'No, not like Wolf Heart," she told him fearfully. "He does not play tricks like you." He saw her shudder.

"What do you mean?"

"That wolf who attacked you."

"What about it?"

"It was Wolf Heart!"

He laughed, astonished at her credulity.

"Do not laugh. I did not shoot at a wolf. It was Wolf Heart I shot at. I missed, but his back was red with blood from your knife wounds."

"It was almost dark by then, Running Moon. I can believe you thought you saw Wolf Heart, but what you saw was a shadow, or a tree. You were excited and cannot be sure what you saw. Such things cannot be in this world."

She sighed, reached out, and took him in her arms. "You are a white man. You do not understand such things—even the famous Golden Hawk does not understand. But you are my husband. That is enough."

Unable to still the fire in his loins any longer, he kissed her for a long, delicious moment, then covered her nakedness with his own. Her mouth opened to receive his probing tongue while she spread wide her long legs in order to take him into her. Without needing to guide himself, he entered her hot moistness easily. She laughed deeply, seductively, and tightened her arms about his neck. Her inner muscles pulled him deeper into her. Straddling her on his knees, he put his hands under her small buttocks and lifted her so that he could plunge into her still deeper. As he did so, she groaned and began to twist and lift under him, grunting in sheer, animal pleasure as he drove her to a climax.

Entwined, lost completely in the urgency of their lovemaking, they spoke no more of cannibal owls and medicine men that night.

Jumping into the water, Hawk waded alongside the dugout, then dragged it up onto the embankment and into the willows. Less than a week before, he and Running Moon had fashioned the dugout from a cottonwood log, hollowing it out by hand. That morning Hawk had been inspecting his beaver traps. Carrying his rifle, three fresh pelts, and the broad flat tails they both relished for their sweet meat, he proceeded across the lower meadow, passing the nearly completed cabin, then up the timbered slope to the lodge.

There was no smoke coming from the tepee's flap. Running Moon had let the fire go out. That was odd. She was not a woman to be that careless. Hawk sensed danger. His nerve ends tingling, his belly tightening, all he could think of was Running Moon.

Dropping his traps and the pelts, he covered the last part of the slope in a crouch, slipping cautiously from tree to tree. Keeping his powder horn at the front, he popped two lead balls into his mouth. A third was in place with its charge of powder secured by a tallow-greased patch already firmly seated.

At the edge of the timber, Hawk waited, puzzled. He smelled nothing, heard nothing. But something was wrong. Had Indians attacked? Could a prowling animal have driven Running Moon away?

"Running Moon," he called. "Are you there?"

There was no answer, only the dismal echo of his call. He studied the tepee. About six pelts hung outside near the entrance, stretched on willow hoops to dry, the flesh side turned up to the sun, all of them undisturbed. Dropping back into the woods, Hawk circled cautiously through the timber until he came out behind the lodge.

A side had been torn open. He was about to

call again when he heard a heavy thumping and growling coming from within the lodge. Someone or some animal was inside it, trampling and smashing everything in sight. Hawk thought of Running Moon then and felt a deep, wild anger.

He stepped out of the timber. At the same time a full-grown male grizzly burst through the gaping hole in the tepee and with a fearsome roar charged him. Hawk lifted the Hawken to his shoulder in one swift, fluid movement and fired. The lead ball crashed into the bear's left eye, ranged through its brain, and blew out the back of its head.

The grizzly was dead, only it did not yet know this. Still it came toward Hawk, the momentum of its charge hardly slowing at all. Hawk unsheathed his bowie and stepped toward the onrushing grizzly, eager to finish off the beast with a stroke to its heart. But the bear sagged to the ground a few yards in front of him, then sprawled over onto its side, its mouth gaping open, its remaining eye already dull in death.

Hawk ran past the grizzly to the tepee and stepped through the hole. Running Moon was crumpled to one side, half-buried under an avalanche of gear and provisions. She was still alive and moved slightly as he knelt beside her. He pulled off the bundles of thong-bound beaver plews, then the cooking utensils and other gear. What remained of her dress clung to her in bloody strips. He pushed them aside as gently as he could and saw the great, mishapen welts, the spreading black-and-blue marks, the long, deep slashes left in her silken skin by the bear's razor-sharp talons. Her breathing came in short, painful gasps, and she was holding one hand up to her chest, groaning slightly at each intake of breath.

In his rage the bear had trampled her, snapping bones, crushing organs. She was bleeding internally, he realized, and probably had sustained so many broken bones that she could not move without excruciating pain. She could not possibly last, he realized.

"Running Moon," he whispered, "are you in great pain?"

"Yes. But it will soon pass."

He reached out and laid a hand on her brow, unable to trust himself to speak.

"You see," she whispered. "It is as I feared. The shadow of that bear came back for his skin."

He had no heart to tell her this was foolish talk, that it was a real grizzly that had done this to her and not the shadow of that other one whose skin she had tanned.

"Take me back to my people," she said. "I do not wish my bones to rest alone in this place."

He nodded dumbly, unable to speak, tears scalding his eyes. She closed her eyes and seemed to drop off. For a moment he thought she was gone, but then her eyes opened and she gazed fearfully up at him.

"Be careful, husband," she whispered softly. "Wolf Heart is a fearsome enemy."

"I'll be careful."

She looked past him, out through the hole in the tepee, and her eyes grew clouded, her lids heavy. "I go now," she whispered, "to the Sandhills."

Her eyes closed and her head swung down slackly, her face coming to rest on the tepee's littered floor.

The rest of that day and night he spent sitting on a log by the stream below the cabin, smoking his pipe. At dawn, his grief still shuddering through him like a fever, he burned the cabin he had begun, then salvaged what he could from the tepee, burned that, and fashioned a travois onto which he bound Running Moon's shrouded body.

After this he built a bonfire and burned the bearskin robe thoroughly, poking at it and flipping patches of it open until the flames had reduced the entire robe to ashes. Then he mounted up and started back to Running Moon's village, already dreading the grief he would be bringing to her father's lodge.

— 7 —

Like a cavalry of mounted grizzly bears, the brigade of mountain men rode out of the timber and surrounded Hawk, Joe Meek in the lead. Pulling up, Hawk regarded the silent circle of men. Counting twenty-two men in all, Hawk waited calmly, watching Joe Meek. So far, this was his party.

Joe Meek's small black eyes flicked over the shrouded figure strapped to the travois. A questioning frown on his face, he turned back to Hawk.

"Running Moon," Hawk said.

Joe Meek accepted this statement without comment, then turned about in his saddle to address his followers. "Rest easy, you oversized, lice-ridden brutes," he told them, grinning. "This here's Golden Hawk. He's takin' his woman back to Elk Head's village. Ain't no harm in that."

Then Meek swung back around to face Hawk.

"You won't find the old chief there," he advised Hawk. "And not any other braves—not any that's old enough to fight, that is."

"Where are they?"

"On their way to Brett's Fort to clean it out, with Empson and his hired cutthroats leading the expedition."

"I thought Elk Head drove them away."

"They came back with more liquor—good liquor this time, right out of the king's cellar. I was still at the Blood village when they began distributing it. I tried to convince Elk Head to stay away from the stuff, but the temptation was too great and he joined in with the other bucks. That's when I sent a buddy of mine to warn the fort, then pulled out and rode to Fort Union for help."

"Why the sudden change of heart? Last I knew, you were working for the Hudson's Bay Company."

"You also knew I quit."

"That doesn't explain what you were doing with those bastards in the first place."

"Empson was a fool. He took me on as a scout without knowing who I was. I went along to find out what the Hudson's Bay Company was up to. I found out."

Hawk was thinking now of Long Tom and Angus and Kathleen MacLennan—and all the others in the wagon train. There was a good chance they might no longer be at Brett's Fort, but the way their luck had been going so far, there was also just as good a chance they were still there, waiting for that other wagon train to catch up to them. They would make a real tempting target for these Indians.

"I promised Running Moon I'd return her to her people for burial," Hawk told Joe Meek. "I still must do that. Tell me where you plan to intercept the Blackfoot and I'll meet you there."

"You know Wood's Hole?"

"Yes."

"We'll try to catch them there. If we can't, we'll go on to the fort."

Hawk nudged his horse past Joe Meek and through the ranks of mountain men. They were a wild-looking, motley band of adventurers. Some wore floppy hats, others beaver and ermine caps. Bearskins with the fur exposed were cut into thick, outer vests for some, while others had slung buffalo robes over their shoulders. They possessed all manner of weapons, from hatchets to knifes, from pistols to sawed-off rifles. None of them was sheared, their unruly hair extending clear to their shoulders. Most of them had beards so thick and untended that the only thing truly individual about any of them was their keen eyes, some blue, some dark brown, some hazel—and all of them grim.

They pulled their horses back to give Hawk room, but wasted no words in greeting as they watched him pass by. Joe Meek's shout galvanized them, and in a moment the mountain men had vanished into the forest after him.

The sisters of Running Moon became so upset when they undid the shroud and gazed upon her torn body that they began tearing at Hawk's thighs with their hooked fingers, while some screamed and pounded furiously upon his horse. As the startled horse reared, Hawk slashed through the ropes holding the travois to his saddle, then spurred out of the village. Some small boys, screaming insults and sending undersized arrows after him, chased him as far as their little legs could take them. Not until Hawk was well out of the village did their shrill curses and the wail of the grieving women fade completely.

Hawk reached Wood's Hole early the next morning and found it deserted. Joe Meek's brigade of mountain men left plenty of sign, however, and Hawk followed it until midday, when he crested a ridge and caught sight of a tributary of the Snake River winding through a long valley below him. Alongside the river was Brett's Fort, a sprawling cluster of log buildings surrounded by the tepees and shacks of Blanket Indians. No palisades yet enclosed the fort, despite the abundance of timber on the nearby mountain slopes. Hawk was too far away to see much else, but he thought he caught the gleam of canvas-topped wagons at the fort's entrance.

When he reached the valley floor, a low, pine-studded ridge blocked out the fort, and not until he got to the stream did he get a good look at the fort once more. That was when the rattle of rifle fire broke out and the war cries of the attacking Blackfoot. Lashing his horse to a gallop, Hawk saw that a line of overturned wagons had creted a breastwork behind which the fort's defenders were now firing on the charging Blackfoot.

From Hawk's vantage point, things appeared to be going well as the fire from the wagons took its toll on the hard-charging Blackfoot. And then Hawk saw Joe Meek's mountain-man contingent charging around to the rear of the fort to meet the crowd of men from the Hudson's Bay Company who were breaking through the fort's rear perimeter. When the two forces met, Hawk realized, there would be havoc in the fort's rear. And if those cutthroats from the Hudson's Bay were able to break through, the settlers would be finished.

Still riding at full tilt, Hawk overtook the charging Blackfoot from the rear. He cut down one Blackfoot directly in his path with a single round from his rifle and knocked another off his horse with a shot from his pistol. Before the Blackfoot could figure out what was happening, Hawk had swept on past them, his head down so as not to get hit by the defenders. As he charged into the fort, a single arrow whizzed past his right shoulder as his horse cleared a pair of wagon traces. Hawk leapt from his saddle and crouched down behind one of the overturned wagons. He found himself beside one of the settlers he and Long Tom had come upon earlier.

"Jed Thompson," the settler exclaimed. "Where in hell did you come from?"

"Never mind that," Hawk replied as the ranks of charging Blackfoot kept on. "Keep firing!"

Ramming home a fresh charge, Hawk spotted a mounted Blackfoot coming straight for their wagon, and squeezed the trigger. The Indian sagged in his saddle, then slipped off his horse. Another Blackfoot overtook him, swept him up onto his horse, and raced back through the still charging ranks of Blackfoot. Reloading swiftly, Hawk could easily have cut down this second Blackfoot, but he had recognized him as Running Moon's father, Elk Head.

"Nice shooting," the settler alongside him cried as he coolly shot another Blackfoot off his horse.

The fire coming from the settlers farther down the line was just as deadly, and the Blackfoot began to mill in front of the wagons, unwilling to continue the charge. One of the braves took the initiative and, waving his coup stick defiantly, led the Indians back out of the settlers' range.

The frontal charge had been broken, but the attack was not over yet. There was still the contingent of Hudson's Bay men coming at them from the rear.

"Where's Angus?" Hawk asked the settler beside him.

"I don't know."

"What about Long Tom?"

"He's over there." The settler pointed to another wagon farther down the line.

Hawk got to his feet and ran over to it. Long Tom was happily loading up, the gleam of combat in his eyes. One glance at Hawk and his grin widened. "What kept you?"

"Never mind that. The Hudson's Bay men are trying to break through from the rear."

"Son of a bitch," Long Tom cried, scooting out from under the wagon.

At Long Tom's shout, Angus hurried over. Hawk told them what he had seen, and for a moment the three men were undecided what to do. They dared not leave this post for fear the Blackfoot would mount another charge. The Blackfoot decided the issue for them.

With a great shout, they attacked—but this time with a difference. Elk Head was in the lead, along with two others—chiefs also, judging from their war bonnets. But instead of attacking the wagons while spread out in a long, vulnerable line of mounted warriors, they stayed in a long file behind their three chiefs and, as they charged, were careful not to fan out. It was sure death for the chiefs, but it would gain time for those warriors in the rear to approach the wagons unscathed. Only then—a few yards from the wagons—would the warriors fan out to overwhelm the wagons.

Ignoring the fierce fire directed at them by the settlers, Elk Head and the two chiefs rode closer, waving their coup sticks defiantly. For a while it appeared as if the three chiefs were protected by some invisible shield. Then the chief on Elk Head's right hand took a shot in the chest, sagged, and slipped from his mount. A moment later the chief on the other side of Elk Head took a round in the skull and toppled backward off his horse.

Two warriors from the rear immediately took the place of the fallen chiefs. Unwilling to kill Elk Head, a man he admired so much and the father of a woman he would never forget, Hawk nevertheless raised his rifle and centered his

sights on the Blackfoot chief. He was almost relieved when he saw the front of Elk Head's chest
explode as someone else's round found its mark.
Elk Head slipped from his horse.

By this time, the sound of battle was heating
up to their rear. Hawk glanced back and saw the
mountain men caught up in a wild melee with
the Hudson's Bay attackers. Twice Hawk caught
sight of Joe Meek darting about with his pistol
and a short dagger. Some of the Hudson's Bay
men were still on horseback, but most of them
had been dragged from their saddles by this time
and were now on foot, fighting hand-to-hand with
the defenders. Suddenly, a group of the Hudson's Bay attackers fought past the encircling
mountain men and made a run for the rear of the
wagons.

Leaving Long Tom, Hawk gathered together
four defenders, including Angus MacLennan, and
hurried to intercept them. Once within range,
they knelt and opened fire. Though they were
outnumbered by the attackers, their fire was
enough to bring down three of them. By then
Meek and his men, having disposed of the rest of
Thomas Empson's brigands, were hurrying to join
Hawk and Angus MacLennan. Caught in the pin-
cers, the attackers raced off, every man for
himself.

Hawk sent a round into the rear end of one of
those fleeing and was pleased to observe the man
clasp his ass and disappear into the brush.

"Look," Angus cried, pointing.

Hawk spun. The Blackfoot were overwhelming

the wagons, their horses leaping through the gaps between them, warriors flinging themselves off their mounts to engage the settlers in hand-to-hand combat.

"Let's go," cried Joe Meek, waving his mountain men onward.

The Hudson's Bay men no longer a threat, Meek and his men rushed across the grass to join in the combat with the Blackfoot, and Hawk soon found himself face-to-face with a painted Blackfoot, warding off his war club as Hawk plunged his bowie deep into the warrior's groin. Flinging the dead man aside, Hawk spun another brave around and sank the blade of his hatchet into his skull. He did not have time to withdraw it before another Blackfoot bowled into him from the side, driving him to the ground. As Hawk tried to roll away, the Indian pinned Hawk's forearms with his knees and raised his war club over his head.

A shot from behind the brave exploded his face outward, the bloody mess spilling onto Hawk. But he paid no heed as he jumped up to see Joe Meek lowering his pistol, a grin on his small, impish face. Hawk nodded his thanks and took off after a Blackfoot scrambling into the rear of one of the wagons. Overtaking him, Hawk looked beyond the warrior and saw a settler's wife with two wild-eyed tots squealing in terror under her skirt. The woman was staring with grim fury at the painted savage reaching out for her, a huge pistol gleaming in her hand. As Hawk ducked low to get out of her line of fire, she shot the Blackfoot's face, twisting away in horror as she saw what she had done to him. Hawk dragged the dead Indian from the wagon and whipped around, ready for more action.

But it was all over. Finished.

The few remaining Indians still within the fort hopped aboard their mounts and raced back through the wagons, some holding bloody scalps, all of them *ki-yiing* like children just let out of school. The weary defenders straightened up and watched them go, grateful that they had been able to beat the Indians back this time, but grimly aware that this would not be the last battle between themselves and the red men.

Joe Meek walked up to Hawk. "We decided we didn't have time to wait for you at Wood's Hole," he explained, "not when we saw how bad things looked. We snuck into the fort last night, right under the Indians' noses. I figured you'd get here all right. And you did. Neat trick that, joining the Blackfoot charge."

"I didn't see any other way."

"When I saw it was you, I told everyone to hold their fire." He grinned. "I think one or two heard me."

A tall gentleman in a tie and long frock coat and wearing a beaver hat with a hole in the crown walked up to them. He was dragging by the nape of his neck none other than Thomas Empson. The Englishman from Ottawa was in terrible shape, his bloody knees sticking out of his pants, his vest bloody, his hat gone. He looked about ready to cry, and when the tall gentleman kicked him so hard he went sprawling before Joe Meek and Hawk, tears slid down his begrimed face.

Ignoring Empson, Joe Meek introduced the tall gentleman to Hawk. "This here's Bill MacWhirter," he told Hawk, "the gent who's building this tradin' post. He's a partner in the American Fur Company. Bill, meet Jed Thompson."

Hawk shook the tall man's hand and found it bony and prodigiously strong.

Then all of them turned their attention to Thomas Empson.

"Get up," Joe Meek said to him.

Instead, Empson groveled, his face down, a terrible mewling sound coming from his throat.

"Get up or I'll take your scalp," Meek roared.

Shakily, Empson pushed himself upright. He was trembling in sheer terror. The sight of a man so craven made every one of them sick to their stomachs. How, they wondered, could a man this spineless have been able to arouse the terrible Blackfoot?

"We ain't goin' to kill you, Empson," said MacWhirter.

"That's ... that's mighty decent of you, Bill."

"Bill's right," Joe Meek agreed. "Wouldn't be fittin', killing the likes of you."

Empson moistened dry lips and nodded gratefully. He looked ready to fling himself at their feet in sheer gratitude.

"What we're goin' to do instead is give you a horse," said MacWhirter, "and send you back to Ottawa, or whatever hole you crawled out of. How's that sound?"

"A horse?"

"That's right."

"I can't ride," Empson cried, quivering with apprehension. "I'll need a wagon to drive, or a buggy. Provisions. A guide."

Joe Meek shook his head. "Sorry. We can't spare none of that. But we'll make sure the horse we give you is still alive."

At once Thomas Empson understood what his fate was. "You can't do that! I'll get lost out there. I won't make it back."

"More'n likely."

"It's the same thing as murder."

"We'll give you a pistol with one lead ball. Maybe you can find a use for it if the Crow or the Bannock get a hold of you. We ain't entirely heartless."

The man began to cry. In disgust Joe Meek grabbed him and flung him away, telling one of the mountain men to pen him up until they could find a horse for him.

Angus MacLennan came running. "It's Long Tom," he gasped, stopping in front of Hawk. "He's asking for you, Jed."

Kathleen MacLennan was with Long Tom. His head was resting in her lap and she was gently smoothing back his hair. Directly over his heart, the broken shaft of a Blackfoot arrow protruded from his ribs. It was obvious that any attempt to remove the arrowhead would bring a freshet of blood after it—and with it Long Tom's instant death. Never had Hawk seen a man still alive look as pale as Long Tom, or as peaceful. As

Hawk settled beside him, Long Tom reached out and took his hand.

"Looks like I won't be going back to my cabin for those notes, after all."

At once Hawk recalled what Long Tom had told him about the journal he had been keeping during the years he had spent in the West, notes concerning the flora, the fauna, the spectacular natural beauty of the Rocky Mountains.

"That's too bad, Tom."

"But you'll be going back."

"Me?"

"Will you do it for me, Hawk?"

"You sounded pretty proud of the way that cabin of yours is hid. You'll have to give me pretty good instructions for finding it."

"I already thought of that. I have a map. You won't have any trouble finding the cabin. Now, will you do it for me?"

Hawk did not hesitate. "Yes."

Long Tom seemed enormously relieved. A little color actually returned to his face. "I made some additional notes these past weeks, Hawk. I want you to take them. They're in my saddlebags."

"What'll I do with them, Long Tom? Who do you want me to give them to?"

"My father in Cambridge, Hawk, Algernon Percival Farrington, Junior. He will see to it that my journal gets published. I am certain of it."

Long Tom looked away from Hawk then, and his head sagged back onto Kathleen's lap. His gaunt face was now almost bluish in color. He smiled wanly and closed his eyes. All this time he had been holding Hawk's wrist. Now his grip eased and Hawk felt his hand fall away.

A second later Kathleen gasped and began to cry as the sudden, leaden coldness in Long Tom's body revealed his ghost's passing.

"Winter's coming on," Kathleen told Hawk, her hair blowing in the sudden, chill wind. She and Hawk were leaning back against the Widow Martin's wagon while Hawk finished smoking the clay pipe Elk Head had given him.

"You got a month or so yet before the heavy snows set in," Hawk replied.

"The other wagon train still hasn't arrived. No doubt it's Indian trouble.

"Could be. There's plenty of Blackfoot about."

"And Bannocks."

Hawk pulled on his pipe. The campfires were pulsing eyes of light in the surrounding mantle of darkness. Stars gleamed overhead. Locusts filled the night with their throbbing. It was only a day after the burials—not only Long Tom's, but more than six other settlers, including a twelve-year-old girl everyone had loved.

The wagons had been righted and now formed a line alongside the trading post and the four log storehouses that comprised the fort. Already, with the aid of the settlers and the mountain men, a beginning had been made on constructing a palisade to protect the fort. Almost twenty freshly cut logs had been piled up neatly along one perimeter of the fort's boundary.

"Anyway, we can't winter here, Jed, so we'll

have to move on through South Pass before the month is up."

Hawk shrugged. It seemed a prudent-enough course of action. The silence grew between them. Kathleen was evidently hoping he would speak up, fill the silence with an offer to help them—possibly even take them through the pass. But Hawk kept the pipe stem in his mouth and said nothing.

"Jed," she said at last, "we want you to take us the rest of the way."

"I don't know the trails West. I've never been there, and I've never tried to lead a line of wagons in any direction."

"There's always a first time. You know these mountains."

"I don't know, Kathleen. That's quite a responsibility."

"Jed, we can't make it without you."

"That's crazy talk. There's plenty of mountain men around who know this country as well or better than I do. Ask one of them."

"It's you we want. We've been discussing it and we took a vote. John Barley says we don't need you, but he was outvoted. You *must* help us, Jed."

"It'll only bring the Blackfoot down on you—or the Bannock."

"If that happens, you'll make them very sorry."

Hawk was licked and he knew it. "Dammit, Kathleen," he grumbled, "I can't promise anything. Remember, Joe Meek and I are going back to pick up Long Tom's notes and see that they get shipped back East. I promised Tom, and I intend to keep my word."

"But after that, you can return to us here."

"I can't make any promises, Kathleen."

"But you'll try?"

"I'll try—but that isn't a promise."

"Well, it's good enough for me!"

Kathleen's eyes glowed with pleasure. It was as if she had not heard him say he could not make promises or that all he could do was try. She refused to see how unlikely it was he would ever return to the wagon train.

John Barley strode up. Completely healed from his earlier wound, he had acquitted himself admirably during this last action. He met Hawk's gaze; his shoulders were thrust back, his dark eyes flashing defiance.

"I want you to know, Jed Thompson," he said, "that if you do not take this train over the divide to Oregon, it will not matter to me—and to many others. I am quite capable now of taking command, and will do so if the occasion demands."

"That's nice to know."

Barley smiled grimly. "Yes, isn't it?" Then he strode past them, as sassy as a cock after a good morning with the chickens.

"I think I hate that man," Kathleen said.

"He's got a chip on his shoulder, that's for sure. But he's got the balls to get you all over the divide. I wouldn't underestimate him."

"I don't underestimate him. I just don't like him."

Hawk pushed himself away from the wagon.

Kathleen reached out to restrain him. "Where are you sleeping tonight?" she asked softly.

"In my sleeping bag, out near them new cut logs, more than likely."

"No. Stay here with me."

"With you?"

"I don't want to sleep alone—not tonight."

He took his pipe out of his mouth. "When you put it like that, how's a man to refuse?"

She flung her arms around his neck and drew him close to her. The heat of her body almost scalded him. He kissed her, long and deeply, and when the kiss was done, he allowed her to pull him up after her into the wagon. Hester Martin was behind the draped blanket, snoring softly but steadily—a tune Hawk had heard before.

A moment later he dropped to the mattress beside an already naked Kathleen MacLennan. It was not easy keeping his urgency under control as Kathleen kissed him eagerly, her lips opening to his, working slowly, hungrily. He ran his hand down her back, then under her to the warm moisture between her trembling thighs. She groaned softly as Hawk parted them with his knees. Rolling gently onto her, he moved up slightly and slipped into her with amazing ease.

She gasped and clung to him fiercely, her thighs locked about his waist as she lunged upward. In a moment they were both flinging themselves at each other, surging toward release, the wagon floor squeaking wildly under them. When they came, Kathleen gasped, shuddering delightedly.

Afterward, he stayed inside her, feeling her

inner muscles tightening around his bigness. Erect again almost immediately, he pulled her roughly up under him until he was once more pounding into her sweet, lubricious depths. She laughed, delighted, and ran her hands feverishly through his thick golden hair.

This time, without the savage urgency of a moment before, they began to move rhythmically as their sweaty, heaving flesh got better acquainted. Before long Kathleen was moaning aloud, her fingernails raking down his back. Again she shuddered convulsively under him, her arms tightening so fiercely around his neck that he thought for a moment she was going to snap his windpipe. At last, uttering a high, sharp cry—one that must have awakened Hester Martin and the rest of the settlers—she climaxed.

Barely able to breathe, Hawk kept on thrusting. Kathleen's cry died and she lay back, tiny beads of perspiration on her breasts, then began to laugh softly, as if she were tasting something incredibly delicious. Thrusting upward again, she groaned aloud with unashamed pleasure now, her eyes closed, great panting breaths coming from her open mouth.

Raking his back with her nails, she flung herself upward and climaxed again, clinging to him, trembling from head to foot. To prevent her from crying out a second time and waking up the entire Blackfoot country, Hawk covered her lips with his. She squealed softly and tried to pull free. He felt her teeth nipping into his upper lip and then the blood flowing down his chin. It was enough to send him off once more. He slammed down hard into her, pounding and grinding her backside into the hard wagon floor beneath them; then he came in one single, powerful explosion—as if his erection had been a stick of dynamite he had just detonated.

He sagged down upon her, his cheek resting on her breast. Sighing, she ran her hands through his hair. A glow of perspiration covered her face and neck, her breasts. He nibbled on one of her nipples for a while, then pulled back, fully contented.

"That was so nice, Jed," Kathleen murmured dreamily. "Thank you."

"No thanks needed," Hawk said, grinning at her. "I'm glad I pleasured you." He rolled gently off her and lay on his back, gazing up at the canvas ceiling. He could hear clearly the Widow Martin's heavy, regular breathing on the other side of the blanket curtain. She could probably have slept through another Blackfoot attack.

To his surprise he found himself thinking, not of Kathleen but of Running Moon. In his mind's eye she appeared before him as she had on their last night together, her cheeks rouged with red ocher, her body and garments scented with the perfumes she made from dried flowers and the needles of sweet pine. She had filled their lodge with the scent of her presence, and he could see her eyes looking down at him once again, as dark and mysterious as the perfume in her hair.

He stopped himself. It did him no good to think of Running Moon. She was dead. Gone.

And he was now lying with another woman—a white woman, one as filled with passion and desire as Running Moon.

Clearing her throat softly, Kathleen said, "Are you thinking of someone else, perhaps?"

Hawk was astonished at her words. He decided the best course for him was to say nothing.

"Is it that Indian woman, Running Moon?" Kathleen persisted.

"I'd rather not say."

She laughed lightly. "Then it *was* her."

"I'm sorry. It just happened."

"I don't mind, Jed. I can imagine how much you loved—and perhaps still love—Running Moon. There's nothing wrong with that."

She threw a blanket over him, then wrapped one around her shoulders and turned away from him. In less than a minute she was asleep and he was left to stare up at the canvas and wonder at the nature of the strange, tempestuous white woman beside him.

There was no plumb line long enough, it seemed, to sound the depths of a woman's heart.

— 8 —

Fording a creek, Hawk and Joe Meek found Thomas Empson dead, lying in the shallows. They had just released him the day before. They pulled him up onto the shore and rolled him over. He had not been scalped, but an arrow was embedded in his chest. A look of pure surprise remained on his bloated face. Hawk glanced up, looking for his horse, and caught sight of pony tracks farther along the embankment.

He left Joe Meek with Empson's body and followed the tracks. In a patch of willows, he found a Blackfoot's body slumped facedown in a patch of willows. Rolling him over, Hawk saw the Indian's eyes flicker and jumped back just as the Blackfoot flung his bowie up at him.

As the knife soared past him into the brush, Hawk brought his foot down on the Blackfoot's windpipe. At once the Indian lay perfectly still, his obsidian eyes regarding Hawk with cold terror. Taking his foot off the Indian's throat, Hawk saw that the Blackfoot had been shot in the center of his chest. It was clear the lead ball had not exited and was probably still lodged somewhere behind his ribs.

Thomas Empson had made good use of the single round in the pistol Joe Meek had provided for him.

Hawk leaned close to the Blackfoot and, grabbing his hair, pressed his knife against his scalp line. In the Blackfoot's tongue Hawk asked the brave if the White Lodge Blackfoot were done with taking orders from the Hudson's Bay Company.

Wincing, the brave nodded.

Joe Meek came up and stood looking down at the wounded Blackfoot. "How many chiefs did you lose in the attack on the fort?" he asked the Indian.

"Many."

"How many?"

"As many as the fingers on one hand. Maybe more."

"Does Elk Head still live?" Hawk asked, relaxing his hold somewhat.

"No. He has gone to the Sandhills with the other chiefs."

"And Wolf Heart?"

"Wolf Heart stay in his lodge. There he make much magic to help us stay alive."

"Doesn't seem to me he did such a good job."

"His medicine save many braves."

Hawk sheathed his knife and stepped back. "Go," he said.

Hope flared in the Indian's eyes. With a cry, he leapt to his feet, turned, and crashed through the brush. He went only a few strides before crashing headlong. Hawk came up behind him and very cautiously kicked him over.

The Blackfoot had gone far—all the way to the Sandhills.

They reached Long Tom's cabin without incident four days later, following scrupulously the map he had left. Long Tom had been right: only the grizzlies would know his place. It was built on a ledge under a rock overhang. A thick grove of pine and aspen blocked the entrance so that anyone approaching from the trail that ran under it would have no idea of its presence. Meanwhile, more than enough sunshine could slant in under the overhang to warm the cabin.

The cabin itself was spacious, with two bedrooms. The huge living room contained a massive fireplace that covered the kitchen end of it. Off the kitchen was a storeroom and an attached outhouse. Studying this last convenience, Hawk saw where Tom had constructed a small doorway at the base to allow the night soil collected over the winter to be spread elsewhere.

Long Tom's notes were just where he had left them: in a large steamer trunk at the foot of his bed. As soon as night fell and they got a good fire going in the fireplace, the two men dragged the trunk into the living room, opened it, and began piling the manuscripts onto the table. Hawk was troubled at how heavy the foolscap pages were, bound inside heavy portfolio covers.

"Let's see what we got here," Joe Meek muttered eagerly, opening one of the journals.

Joe Meek's begrimed finger ran swiftly underneath the neat, pen-and-ink sentences as he read swiftly down the page, Hawk reading silently along with him. Joe Meek was as good a reader as Hawk, and neither had any trouble keeping together as they read. After finishing the third page, Joe Meek straightened up and stood back away from the table.

"I knew all that about them animals," he said. "But Tom sure put it down with all the i's dotted and t's crossed. He sure didn't leave nothing out that I could see."

Hawk nodded. He was impressed. Long Tom was a born naturalist, and Hawk could understand perfectly why he had worked so hard on these observations of the mountain land's wild creatures and plants. Though much of what Long Tom had discovered was clear enough to Joe Meek and himself, there were thousands of people back East who had never laid eyes on a wolverine or a cougar, and who never would. Only through Long Tom's observations would they ever know the truth about these wild creatures and the land they inhabited.

Joe Meek straightened up and stretched. Hawk leafed through a few more pages, then found something interesting.

"Listen to this, Joe," he said.

Joe took out his pipe and sprawled in a chair by the fire. "I'm listenin'."

". . . and though some naturalists insist on perpetuating such a foolish notion," Hawk read, "I can say with assurance that the wolverine does not leap down from trees onto the backs of bears or elk and other large animals and cling to their backs, killing them in spite of the animal's desperate efforts to be rid of its attacker by running at full speed or rolling over onto it. We need go no further than the formation of the animal itself to prove how foolish are such assumptions. The wolverine's body, legs, feet, and claws are shaped similarly to the black bear, but its claws are somewhat longer and straighter in proportion, and, like the bear, its claws are blunted at the points. This would make it impossible for the wolverine to cling to the back of a fleeing elk or deer. Furthermore, as to another mistaken notion, the wolverines do not den up in the winter like the bear. Instead, they ramble about through the meanest winters, staying close by open streams whenever they find them, even in the highest mountain valleys . . ."

Hawk looked at Joe Meek. "Seems like Long Tom knew a damn sight more about wolverines than most of us, especially them gents with the stiff collars back East."

Joe Meek puffed for a while on his pipe, then got up, dug into the woodbox, and placed more logs on the fire. Returning to the table, he spun a chair around, straddled it, and leaned his chin over it, drawing on his pipe all the while. The air over his head became filled with swirling clouds of fragrant pipe smoke.

"Maybe so," Joe Meek allowed carefully. "And maybe them fancy naturalists back East don't know what they're talkin' about. I never seen one of them out here. No, sir. They wouldn't dare. But, Hawk, once I thought I did see a wolverine on an elk's back. 'Course the elk didn't much like it and the poor son of a bitch kept plowing through the snow until it reached a swift stream and started across. The wolverine was up to it and stayed on its back. The elk never made it all the way across, and when I rode downstream about an hour later, I looked across to the other side and saw that damned wolverine dragging off half the elk's carcass. Seems like that wolverine didn't know it wasn't supposed to be able to do that."

"Could it've been a bear you saw?"

"If so, a small one. And a black bear, not a grizzly."

"Maybe that's what you saw then. Long Tom says here no wolverine could cling to an elk's back; it doesn't have claws sharp enough for it."

Joe Meek smiled and tipped his head just a little. "Ah, but remember what you just read to me. Long Tom said both wolverines *and* bears have them long, blunt claws—so it 'pears to me neither bear nor wolverine should be able to take that ride. Ain't that so?"

Hawk had no answer to that. After all, how could he argue with a man who had Joe Meek's credentials? The incredible tales he had heard from Old Bill Williams concerning the trials and adventures of Joe Meek had curled his hair, until finally Hawk had tended to regard most of the stories as pure fancy. He knew how mountain men liked to stretch a good story clear into the realm of disbelief, then give it one more good kick to make it go even further.

With a shrug, Hawk closed the heavy manuscript and gave up the debate. Besides, he had found reading Long Tom's tiny, meticulous handwriting a difficult chore.

"The problem, as I see it," Joe Meek said, "is getting all these bound manuscripts on that pack horse we brung. It's a long way to Fort Hall from here."

"Put it all back in the trunk, including what we brought from Brett's Fort, then lash the trunk to the pack horse."

"It'd be better if we had an aparejo."

"But we don't."

"We'll do it your way, then."

Suddenly, an arrow came through the side window, shattering the windowpane and slamming into the wall. Another arrow came after it and clattered off the chair Joe Meek had been sitting on. Two more arrows slapped off the tops of the portfolios. Crouching on the floor, both men heard moccasined feet pounding up onto the porch. They flung themselves at the door and managed to drop the latch bar a second before three or four heavy, determined bodies flung themselves against the other side of it.

An arrow shattered the lamp and sent it spinning off the table. It landed with a small explosion that sent flaming oil streaking across the floor and up the wall. Hawk snatched up a bear rug and smothered the flames, while Joe Meek doused the logs in the fireplace with the contents of the bucket resting in the sink, throwing onto the fire both water and the tin plates and cups that had been soaking in it.

Crouched in the sudden inky darkness, Hawk and Joe Meek waited for the Indians to make the next move. It came soon enough as one bold warrior boosted himself in through one of the shattered windows.

"I'll take him," whispered Hawk.

The brave landed on his feet awkwardly, peering around at the cabin's abrupt, pitch-black interior. Keeping low, Hawk glided over, caught the brave's hair, and spun him around. As the Indian came around with his bowie, Hawk grabbed his wrist with both hands, brought it down on his knee, snapping the wrist. As the knife clattered to the floor, Hawk released the Indian and brought up his bowie, sinking it into his stomach, then raking upward as far as he could go.

He heard moccasined feet drop to the floor behind him. He turned. But Joe Meek was behind this second Indian and buried his hatchet in the brave's skull.

"Let's get out there," Hawk told Joe Meek, and boosted himself out through the same window the first Indian had come through. He waited by the window for Joe Meek to follow him out of the cabin, then they left the cabin and moved out of the rocky overhang until they felt pine needles under their feet.

Since they had no idea how many Indians were in this war party, they separated to find out. As Joe Meek glided off into the darkness, Hawk headed for a clump of pine. Reaching it, he heard scuttling in the bushes beside him and turned in time to take a warrior's charge. The force of it slammed him back against a tree.

The brave was intent on turning Hawk's brains to mush with his war club, so Hawk centered his attention on the fellow's right arm, gradually pinning it back against another tree. When he was able to knock the club out of the savage's grasp, he throttled the Indian with both hands, his fingers closing about the fellow's windpipe with the strength of a steel cable.

The brave sank beneath Hawk until Hawk was astride him on the ground, his fingers still tightening. The brave struggled, a terrible fear writ large in his eyes. His tongue protruding grotesquely from his gaping mouth, the Indian sagged, lifeless. Hawk let him fall to the forest floor.

He heard a muffled cry from the other side of the cabin. Running from the pines, Hawk saw a single brave race across the clearing and into the forest. Hawk overtook him just as the warrior reached his pony. As the Indian leapt onto his pony, Hawk grabbed his shoulder in an attempt to pull him off.

The mounted Indian flung around, his long knife flashing. The blade sank deep into Hawk's shoulder. Hawk lost strength in his fingers and released the Indian, who rode off into the night. Hawk was down on one knee, stanching the flow of blood with a portion of his shirt, when Joe Meek ran up to him.

"He get away?"

"Yep," Hawk said.

"Damn it all to hell. I had him in my sights, but he moved just as I pulled the trigger." Then Joe frowned down at Hawk's wound. "You hurt bad?"

"I'll live."

"Them were Comanches."

"I know."

"Was it your tribe, the Antelope band?"

"No. From their war paint, it was the Kotsoteka," said Hawk.

"You mean the Buffalo Eaters?"

"That's right."

"You had much truck with them before this?"

Hawk stood up. He felt a little woozy. "No."

"Then why are they after you?"

"They know of me. Any Comanche who brings in my scalp will be able to purchase a fine wife and will be regarded highly by all the other chiefs. Only good things will happen to him after such a feat."

"My God! That means you got to fight the entire Comanche nation?"

"Only a few at a time, Joe."

"Well, I'm sure glad to hear that."

Hawk looked around him at the dim woodland. "There should be Indian ponies around here somewhere. That last fellow was in no mood to gather the rest of them up. If we find them, we can use them to pack for us. I call this a stroke of good luck."

"You would."

They found the ponies eventually and, taking up their reins, started back to the cabin. As they reached it, Hawk sighed wearily.

"I think we better move out of here, Joe—and fast."

"My thinking exactly," the small mountain man said, pushing into the cabin.

But the knife wound in Hawk's shoulder did not heal all that quickly, and it was a week before Hawk was ready to set out for Fort Hall. Early in the morning they left the cabin without incident, but less than an hour later, Joe Meek pulled up and pointed back along the ridge they had just left. Beyond it, high on the mountain's great flank, a dark plume of smoke was rising into the bright morning sky—smoke from a burning cabin.

"That feller we let get away is keeping himself busy," Joe Meek muttered angrily.

Hawk felt the same anger. That had been a fine cabin Long Tom had built. Frowning with concern, he glanced back at the pack horse carrying the trunk with Long Tom's manuscripts inside. Nothing, he told himself, must prevent them from delivering that trunk.

Two nights later they made a camp by a quiet stream and built a fire. A coffeepot was sitting on a flat rock alongside it, and fresh jerky and beans were sizzling in the frying pan close to the fire. Both men had their pipes out and sat cross-legged, solemnly smoking their pipes while they eased their weary backsides from the day's long drive over rough, inhospitable country. It might have appeared that they had completely forgotten the remaining Comanche. But if the Comanche was nearby and thought so, this would have been a mistake. Each man had his rifle, fully loaded and primed, resting on the ground close beside him. In addition, their knives were sitting loosely in their sheaths.

The scream of the Giant Cannibal Owl shattered the stillness. Hawk spun around just as the stinking body of a dead Indian flew out of the darkness and landed on the campfire, scattering the coffee, the blazing firewood, and the frying pan with their supper in it. Coming right after the dead Indian was a live one, leaping through the air at Hawk. He had a hatchet in one hand and a knife in his teeth like a pirate.

Hawk had sense enough not to stay on his feet. He threw himself flat on the ground, snatched up his rifle, and fired at the Comanche as the Indian sailed past him and struck the ground. The round missed. Without pausing, the Indian flung himself upright and vanished into the darkness beyond the fire.

As Hawk reloaded, he heard again—this time from a greater distance—the cry of the Great Cannibal Owl.

Joe Meek had already righted the coffeepot and was frantically trying to salvage some of the jerky and beans. "Seems like that crazy Indian's got your number, Hawk," he growled unhappily.

"Looks that way, all right."

Hawk finished seating the lead ball inside the rifle barrel. Attaching the hickory rod to the Hawken, he got to his feet and peered cautiously about him at the dark timber. He saw nothing, which did not surprise him. That fool Comanche was already some distance from them by this time.

Putting down the rifle, Hawk and Joe Meek dragged the dead—and now scorched—Indian off into the timber. They found a steep ravine in the darkness, kicked the Indian off into it, and stood waiting for what seemed like hours for the body to stop rolling and crashing through the brush.

They returned to the fire and went on with their supper on the assumption that, crazy though this particular aborigine was, he was not likely to try another surprise so soon after the first.

That night both men slept a good distance from the campfire, while they kept the horses hobbled close beside it so they could keep an eye on them during the night. Each man took turns staying awake. The next morning, red-eyed and irritable, they ate a hasty breakfast and packed the horses to continue the journey to Fort Hall.

Hawk finished tightening the cinch on his saddle and peered past his horse at Joe Meek.

"Joe, I think you better go on alone."

'Why?"

"That Comanche is after me more than he's after you. I'm the one to take him out. It's the best chance we have of getting Long Tom's notes to the fort."

Joe Meek shrugged. "That's your decision to make, but watch out. That hoss is some crazy Injun."

"Just the kind I'm used to," Hawk said. He swung up into his saddle, wound the line to his pack horse around his saddle horn, and rode off.

Cresting a ridge, he turned and waved good-bye to the small, tough mountain man. Then he pushed his horse on up the slope, keeping Joe Meek and his train of pack horses in sight until they vanished at last a half-mile below him. He had been hoping to catch sign of his quarry perhaps slipping through the timber as he stalked Joe Meek and the pack train. But he had seen and heard nothing. This Comanche was a tough one, all right, and Hawk almost regretted the iron necessity that made his death essential.

Almost.

— 9 —

Hawk felt uneasy. This Comanche knew his tricks, especially how to sound like the Great Cannibal Owl. And how to use the bodies of dead Indians to strike terror into an enemy's heart. He wondered, as well, if the Comanche had a reata and had learned to use it as Hawk sometimes did. It was a thought that made him uneasy. He had a weird feeling that his other self—his Comanche self—was tracking him.

He rode on through the timber above the trail, cutting a large circle in an effort to pick up the Comanche's sign, keeping his eyes not only on the ground ahead of him, but on the trees arching over him as well. Late in the afternoon he caught a movement in the thin file of trees to his right. It was only for an instant, but it was enough to alert him. He kept on for a hundred yards more, then dismounted, unsaddled his horse, and removed the packs from his pack horse. Hobbling

139

the two horses in a nearby clearing, he left them and with his Hawken drifted cautiously through the trees, every sense alert.

From his left a twig broke underfoot. Hawk pulled himself swiftly up into the nearest pine and clambered up as high as he could go. When he came to rest, he had a fine view of the ground below and the sloping forest floor beyond. Anyone moving through this thin stand of timber would be spotted at once.

He waited patiently, but no skulking Indian appeared. Near dusk Hawk caught movement some distance away, and peering closely and patiently, his eyes gradually brought into focus the Comanche's pony cropping grass in a clearing. Hawk kept his eyes on it for a long time, hoping it would give him a clue as to the Comanche's whereabouts. But darkness fell over the land without a sign of him. By this time the arches of Hawk's moccasined feet were aching as they sagged around the branches he was standing on. He was beginning to feel a little foolish, waiting so long, high in this pine, for he knew not what.

Did he actually think he *was* the Great Cannibal Owl?

A reata dropped out of the darkness and settled like something alive onto his shoulders. Dropping his rifle, Hawk grabbed hold of the encircling reata a split second before it closed around his neck. From behind and a little above him came a high, stuttering shriek—the demented cry of the Great Cannibal Owl.

The Comanche Hawk had been looking for had

found him. With one swift snap, Hawk was yanked off the branch. His twisting body crashed into a pine. He floundered through branches, the needles cutting into his face like fingernails. Clasping his legs about the tree trunk, Hawk managed to cling to the tree for a moment, but was dragged brutally free of it and sent plunging all the way to the forest floor. At the last moment the reata pulled him up short, almost snapping off his neck. Barely conscious, still clinging to the reata, wound now like a piece of steel wire around his neck, Hawk commenced to swing back and forth, his body slowly twisting.

Despite the strength in his ten fingers, the reata continued to close relentlessly about his neck, threatening to cut off his windpipe within minutes. In a desperate gamble, Hawk allowed his head to drop grotesquely and twist to one side while he kept both eyes barely open.

A great, birdlike apparition swooped down out of the trees and landed beside him, his dark wings fashioned out of pine branches strapped to his shoulders. The Comanche's face was hidden inside the mask of a long-beaked, owlish creature, horrible enough to make even Hawk's skin crawl. What he was getting, Hawk realized, was a dose of his own medicine. As he continued to twist on the end of the Comanche's reata, he starred unblinkingly at the Indian, who stepped close to Hawk in order to inspect his victim's condition.

By this time Hawk should have been dead, and he looked dead enough to the Indian. Apparently pleased with his handiwork, the Indian slowly circled Hawk, who was experiencing periodic blackouts by this time. Despite the fact that he had been able to hold the noose open somewhat with his hands, the reata continued to tighten about his throat.

The Comanche pulled back and abruptly began a victory dance around Hawk, uttering the same preposterous, high-pitched cries Hawk had heard from him earlier. Then, tiring of his dance and not wanting Hawk to go to his reward with all his parts intact, the Comanche stepped forward and drew a long skinning knife from his sheath. Hawk thought the Comanche was about to plunge the knife into Hawk's slowly twisting torso, then go to work on his genitals. Instead, the Comanche sliced through the reata just above Hawk's head.

Hawk crumpled to the forest floor and rolled down the slope, coming to rest finally with his head down, both hands still clutching at the noose about his neck. Carefully, he loosened the reata enough to enable himself to suck in a few painful gulps of air. As blood pounded back into his head, his head spun violently and he blacked out.

He was dimly aware of the Comanche moving toward him from out of the brush beside him. He tried to move his limbs, but his arms and legs were as heavy as stone monuments. Digging his moccasined foot under Hawk's belly, the Comanche kicked Hawk over onto his back. Peering up at him from under nearly shut lids, Hawk saw

that the Indian still had his fool wings strapped
to his shoulders and that he had not yet taken off
his Cannibal Owl mask. In a hand-to-hand fight,
this could not help but work to Hawk's advantage.

Strength was now flowing back into his limbs,
and Hawk still had his bowie sheathed at his
side and his throwing knife was still in its thin
case at the back of his neck.

The Comanche, however, now had a lance with
him and was raising it over his head, intent on
skewering Hawk to the forest floor, a necessary
preliminary to the delights that would follow.
Hawk did not wait. As the Comanche brought
down the lance, he rolled away and sprang to his
feet.

His lance quivering in the ground, the astonished Comanche flung himself toward Hawk.
Hawk ducked aside, then turned and ran into
the timber. He did not run a straight course.
Hoping to use his pursuer's bulky costume to his
own advantage, Hawk zigged and zagged, cutting
between trees less than a foot apart, crashing
through brush and wildberry bushes, not forget-
ting to use small clumps of juniper whenever he
could. He came finally to a shallow stream and
darted across it. Then he crouched behind thick
brush and waited.

By this time, in order to keep up with Hawk,
the Comanche had been forced to leave behind
his clumsy wings, and in order to see where he
was going, he had abandoned his cumbersome
mask. Nevertheless, he was still far enough behind Hawk so that when he reached the stream,

he was forced to pull up in some confusion, unable to find Hawk's tracks.

Able to breathe normally now, all feeling having returned to his limbs, Hawk felt capable of handling this Comanche and was eager to be done with this crazy business. When he saw the Comanche start downstream in the wrong direction, Hawk immediately stood up and cleared his throat.

The Comanche spun about with a cry and charged back up the stream toward Hawk. Too late Hawk saw the pistol in the Comanche's hand. The gun roared. The ball struck the side of Hawk's skull and glanced off. But it had the force of a sledgehammer and slammed Hawk back against a tree. The elated Comanche, his hatchet raised over his head, uttered one more piercing war cry as he gained the bank, then lunged for Hawk.

Leaning against the tree to keep his balance, Hawk reached back, grasped his throwing knife's small blade, and sent it at the Comanche. It sliced into the Indian's windpipe, and Hawk heard the noise a crushed neck bone makes. Gasping, his eyes wide in horror as he found himself unable to breathe, the Comanche stumbled to his knees, blood spurting from his neck. Hawk unsheathed his bowie and scalped him, performing the operation as neatly and as efficiently as his Comanche hosts had taught him—a slice around the hairline with his knife tip, then a quick snap to lift off the scalp intact.

He figured he owed himself this one.

*   *   *

When Hawk opened the flap to the lodge out-side Fort Hall that Joe Meek now called home, the tough little mountain man looked up at him in pure amazement, then anxiety when he saw the white bandage under his hat, the one cover-ing the damage done by the Comanche's lead ball.

"What in hell happened to you, hoss?"

"Ran into an Indian impersonating me," he said, smiling ruefully.

"Well, get in here and let me look at you. I thought for a minute there you might've tangled with one of them wolverines we was arguing about."

"He was a Comanche wolverine," Hawk said, stepping through the opening and striding across the thickly carpeted floor.

As he sat cross-legged on the cushion Joe Meek provided for him, Hawk felt of his face and un-derstood what an impression he must be making to the Indians and traders he had met swarming in and out of Fort Hall. There were still scabbed ridges on his cheeks and forehead where the pine needles had slashed at his face, and there was the black-and-blue rope burn on his neck. Though that Comanche's ball had not penetrated his skull, it still rang like a bell on occasion.

Both men took out their pipes and lit up. As they got their furnaces going and the tepee began to fill up with smoke, Hawk asked Joe Meek if he had had any trouble on the way to the fort.

"Not one bit, hoss. I guess you took care of that

when you went after that Comanche. He the last of them this trip?"

"That's the way it looks."

"You got his scalp?"

"In one of my saddlebags."

"From the look of you, he wasn't no easy Comanche to take."

'He sure as hell didn't roll over like a kitten. The thing was, he must've been talking to a few Blackfoot before he came at me. Some of his tricks were duplicates of what I used on them a while back."

"Oh, hell, I heard all about that, Hawk. Ain't you referring to them pine wings you fashioned and that yell from the treetops, then dropping Indian bodies out of trees."

Hawk pulled the pipe stem out of his mouth and grinned in surprise. "I am."

"Old Bill's the one spreading that tale around," Joe Meek said, chuckling. "And most of the Blanket Indians around these tradin' posts know it by heart. No reason why you shouldn't have a whole flock of crazy Indians trying to pull them same tricks on you. These here redskins enjoy a good laugh as well as we do. Maybe even more."

Hawk said nothing for a while, feeling suddenly as amused as Joe Meek. Sometimes the way word got around from tribe to tribe was uncanny. It was as if news were carried on the air somehow from village to village.

"What about Long Tom's journals?" Hawk asked. "Are they safe?"

"Courtney Walker has taken personal charge of the trunk."

"Walker?"

"He's the new chief factor in charge here. He's been at this fort a month now and looks like he'll do. Served as chief trader on the Oregon coast for ten years."

"Did you tell him about Empson?"

"Yep. He denied all knowledge of him, and I believe the man. Might as well let it go, Hawk. I doubt if the company will try anything that foolish again."

Hawk saw no reason to disagree.

The flap was flung back and a Minnetaree girl not much older than sixteen entered. Hawk had seen her outside tending a pot simmering over a fire. As she stirred its contents, chunks of buffalo meat and roots swirled after her wooden spoon. She placed a hot, steaming bowl of it in front of Hawk. Then came wheat-flour cakes with buffalo marrow for butter, and a large tin cup of steaming coffee. Beside the coffee she placed a small doeskin bag of sugar.

As Hawk picked up the bowl, Joe Meek said something sharp to the girl. She ducked her head unhappily, retreated to the farthest edge of the lodge, and took a seat on her bed of buffalo robes that were laid on a spring of willow sticks. Leaning back against a rawhide-thong backrest, she pulled a robe over her knees and sulked.

"What'd you tell her?" Hawk asked, chomping on the succulent chunks of meat. "This is delicious."

"I asked her what the hell took her so long. You was in here five minutes before she brought in that bowl. She's a mite slow, but she's gettin' there."

"How old is she?"

"Seventeen. Ain't she a pippin?"

"What's her name?"

"Summer Sky. I calls her Sky."

The scent of horsemint and sweet pine that clung to Summer Sky began to permeate the lodge, and as Hawk consumed eagerly the meal she had placed before him, he had difficulty not staring at Joe Meek's recent acquisition.

Summer Sky's dress was of fine doeskin, tanned a light-coffee color. Her skirt reached just below her knees, and along its hemline ran a short fringe decorated with tiny bells. They had jingled softly when she entered. Her belt was intricately beaded with geometrical designs in blue, white, and green. As soon as she was settled on her couch, she threw a light, hairless elkskin robe over her shoulders.

"Hell, Joe," Hawk remarked, grinning across at his host, "I'd say she's pretty enough to be a little slow now and then. How much did she cost you?"

"Those Comanche ponies I trailed in with and twenty cents' worth of beads, and a Green River I been trying to trade for some time."

"Sounds like you lost your head completely."

Joe Meek grinned. "Told myself I'd never take another one. But, like I said, she a real pippin, and I do feel a mite younger now when I go to bed."

Hawk finished the bowl of buffalo stew and nodded at Summer Sky, smiling his pleasure at her cooking skills. She blushed and looked hopefully toward her master, as if to say, "You see, husband, this one isn't at all displeased."

At her glance, Joe Meek melted and spoke softly to Summer Sky in her own tongue. Summer Sky brightened considerably.

Only then, with an unhappy glance at Hawk, did she recount in low, urgent tones what she had been waiting to tell her husband. Watching Joe Meek's expression as he listened, Hawk became somewhat uneasy.

"What's wrong, Joe?" Hawk asked.

"Hawk, ain't your sister livin' with a Shoshone band?"

Hawk nodded. "She's the wife of Crow Wing. But what's that got to do with Summer Sky?"

"Sky knows who you are. And she just heard some Crows boastin'. They rode in this morning to trade some plews they'd just taken in a raid on a Shoshone village."

Hawk came alert. "Go on . . ."

"The Crows were braggin' about how many scalps they took. Names were mentioned. Summer Sky heard something about your sister."

Hawk felt sick. "Annabelle? What about her?"

Joe Meek didn't want to go on, but he had no choice. "It's like this, Hawk. The Crows said they have your sister's scalp, and that she's dead, sure enough, along with most of the other Shoshone in her band. There weren't many captives taken, and the Shoshone village was thoroughly routed. The Crows doin' the braggin' say they don't care if Golden Hawk comes after them for killing his sister. They say they are not like the Blackfoot, who are too foolish and cowardly to stop the white Comanche."

"Where are these Crows?"

"Sky said they left the fort a couple of hours ago."

Hawk stood up. "I'm going after them."

"Not you, hoss. Us. Count me in." Joe Meek got to his feet also. "I wouldn't want to miss this scalping party."

Night had fallen and the four Crow braves had a fire going. A freshly killed mule deer was roasting on a spit over it, which was unusual behavior in itself. Indians seldom waited for fresh meat to cook before devouring it.

Hawk stepped out of the darkness, carrying only his rifle. Since the Crows were fond of swearing that they had never killed a trapper or taken the warpath against settlers moving through their country, Hawk was in no immediate danger. But he could see at once that the Crows knew who he was. Their eyes flicked right and left, looking for any other trappers that might be crouched around them, but the darkness around their fire was an impenetrable curtain.

To look upon these vainglorious savages and to have heard them a moment before still boasting proudly of their attack on Annabelle's Shoshone band filled Hawk with an almost ungovernable fury. That these warriors could feel pride in their murder and rapine sickened him. It was almost more than he could bear. He had to struggle to keep his composure.

Only one of the four Crows got to his feet. He was a tall and strikingly handsome warrior, his braided hair so long it was folded back in heavy queues.

He raised his hand in greeting. "The people of the Absaroka have heard of Golden Hawk's struggle against the Comanche and the Bannock," the Crow said in passable English. "Even the Blackfoot feel his fury. Like this Crow warrior, Golden Hawk is a great hero. He too fights all Indians."

"The Crow are the best horse thieves," Hawk countered. "Even the Comanche say it is hardest of all to steal horses from the Crow."

Pleased at this compliment, the Crow nodded. The formalities over, he straightened and folded his arms on his chest and waited. It was clear he and the others knew that Golden Hawk had heard of the Crow attack on the Shoshone village where his sister lived, and of their boast as well.

"The Crows speak much of their triumphs," Hawk told the Crow, his voice cold, his sharp blue eyes unwavering. "They brag they have taken many scalps and many ponies from a certain Shoshone band."

"You speak the truth," the Crow responded.

"The sister of Golden Hawk was in that Shoshone band."

The Crow made no effort to deny it. "We have

a great victory over the Root Eaters, that filthy band of Shoshone. Our warriors take many coups and many fresh scalps they add to their scalp poles. Now every Crow in our band has new ponies in his string."

"Was my sister killed or taken captive?"

The Crow's face hardened into a proud, arrogant mask. "The woman of Crow Wing was not taken captive, neither was her son."

"Then my sister is dead."

The tall Crow did not smile, but Hawk saw a cruel delight in his lustrous black eyes. "Golden Hawk's sister was but a Shoshone squaw when the Crow warriors destroyed her people and their village. She is dead, Golden Hawk, as is her small son. Be content, Golden Hawk," the tall Crow admonished, his tone close to a taunt. "It is done. There is nothing you can do now."

"I want the scalp of the Crow who took my sister's scalp," Hawk told the Indian.

"He is dead."

"You lie. Send for him. Or I will kill a Crow warrior for every month I wait for him to appear."

Hawk's words stunned the four Crows. They were a proud, strutting tribe of warriors, always eager for glory. So fierce were they in warfare they had stemmed the flow of the Blackfoot south into the Rockies and the plains, and were known to be the only Indians in the Absarokas to war on all tribes indiscriminately. Such a challenge as Hawk hurled at them would have to be taken seriously.

The Crow straightened to his full height and

fixed Hawk with his piercing black eyes. "I am Spotted Tail," he informed Hawk. "Many coups have I taken. I am a very famous chief of my people. Spotted Tail is glad Golden Hawk has heard of the Crow's great victory over the Root Eaters. I, Spotted Tail, will accept Golden Hawk's challenge now."

As Hawk reached down for his bowie, the Crow rushed at him, a large skinning knife flashing in his hand. Hawk deliberately fell backward to the ground, tucked his feet into the Crow's midsection, and flung him headlong. Spotted Tail hurtled at least six feet through the air before striking the ground. Scrambling to his feet, Hawk reached back for his throwing knife and sent it at the Crow. The blade sank into the Crow's chest, but did not stop him. Still brandishing his knife, Spotted Tail rushed upon Hawk.

Bracing himself, Hawk took the Indian's charge, then ducked under his slashing dagger. As the two slammed together, Hawk plunged upward with his bowie, the blade sinking hilt-deep into Spotted Tail's belly. Yanking out the blade, Hawk lifted the Crow high over his head. His pent-up fury taking over at this point, he slammed Spotted Tail to the ground. The Crow struck facedown and began to twist slowly. With one swift, murderous stroke, Hawk kicked in Spotted Tail's temple, then bent down and took his scalp.

A shot came from the darkness. Hawk turned to see a Crow less than a foot from him, his hatchet upraised. He sagged to the ground, Joe Meek's lead ball in his spine. The mountain man stepped out from behind the boulder and leveled two pistols at the remaining Crows.

Hawk glared over at them. He did not know if they could understand English, but he did not care. "I do not want a war with the people of the Absaroka," he told them. Then he brandished the Crow's bloody scalp at them. "But if the Crow wish to wage such a war, I am eager for it."

The two Crows stared at Hawk. They might have understood his words, but there was no way of reading this from the look on their impassive faces.

Joe Meek glanced at Hawk. "We could execute these two murderin' savages right here, and no one would know who killed them."

"You don't understand," Hawk said bitterly. "I *want* the Crow to know I did this."

Retrieving his throwing knife, Hawk gave Joe Meek a nod and stepped back into the darkness, the mountain man cutting ahead of him through the black night. A moment later they came to their horses, mounted up, and started back to Fort Hall.

Taking Spotted Tail's scalp had made Hawk feel a little better, but killing him had done nothing to ameliorate the terrible, crushing sense of loss he now felt.

As they neared Joe Meek's lodge early the next morning, Summer Sky rushed out to greet them. Grabbing the mountain man's hands even before he could dismount, she began to tell him something she obviously thought to be of enormous importance. But the torrent of words poured out of her at such a speed Joe Meek had to roar at her to go slower. Then, listening intently, he looked first incredulous, then astonished.

"What is it, Joe?" Hawk asked, pulling up alongside him.

"You won't believe this, Hawk, but—"

There was no need for Joe Meek to say more. Hawk had already flung himself from his horse and was running to meet a familiar figure who had just emerged from the fort's main gate. It was a tragically reduced woman he saw—but at the sight of her, an awful weight lifted from Hawk's heart.

Annabelle was not dead, after all.

— 10 —

When Annabelle told her story, it was clear why the Crows had mistakenly believed she was dead.

She had not been in the village when the Crow war party attacked. It was washday, and as was her custom, she had chosen to take her family's wash to an isolated bend downstream. The spot she had chosen was screened from the bank by willows and boasted a low sand bar that formed a cozy, isolated beach.

There were no swimmers at this point in the stream, since less than a hundred yards farther on, the surface was broken by a churning patch of rapids as **the stream** began its plunge **toward** the falls beyond. Annabelle loved being near the swift water. The sound it made rushing over the rocks filled the air with a soft, cool murmur, like the wind passing through the tops of pine trees. For Annabelle this hidden spot was perfect. Here, in complete privacy, she could bathe herself while splashing about in the water with her infant son.

She was pounding the dirt out of one of Crow Wing's doeskin shirts with a wooden mallet when she first heard the thunder of stampeding ponies. Pulling back out of the water, she placed Little Birch safely out of sight under the embankment, then climbed up the bank to peer through the birches. A Crow war party was stampeding the Shoshone pony herds away from the village, while mounted Crow warriors swept down on it.

The attackers' war cries and those of the village's defenders rent the air. Shoshone braves rushed from their lodges to meet the Crow in combat. White-haired Shoshone men pulled Crow warriors from their ponies. Shoshone women joined their husbands in the battle, their sharp screams and war cries cutting the air. Even the Shoshone youngsters, small bows in their hands, rushed into the fray. But the Crow were numerous, their ponies swift, and they were fierce and effective warriors.

Annabelle's first thought was of Crow Wing. He would be in the thick of it now, she realized, among the first to rush out to defend their village. Since he was always eager for battle—too eager, in Annabelle's estimation—she could imagine now his joy in combat. To him this meant a chance to accomplish great coups and increase his influence in his band's councils.

So he would fight. And if this Crow war party

was large enough and prevailed, all would be over for this band, and her husband's scalp would soon flutter from a Crow warrior's scalp pole.

In growing alarm, she watched the distant mayhem. The tide of battle was not with the Shoshone defenders. Their lodges were going up in flames. Crow braves were racing after screaming women and children. The old ones were being struck down. The rout was on.

It was bad enough for Annabelle to watch; it was infinitely worse to know there was nothing she could do. Nothing. From this moment on, her chief concern had to be for her son and herself. Tucking the long knife she always carried into her cleft, she felt its blade resting against her skin and was comforted. Then, hugging her swaddled infant to her breast, she darted into the stream and half-swam, half-waded to the other side. Gaining the far bank, she headed across the small clearing toward a timbered slope.

She was only a stride from the timber when a lone Crow on the other side of the stream caught sight of her. Uttering a high-pitched war cry, he lashed his pony across the stream, bounded up into the clearing, and charged across it toward her.

Ducking into the timber, Annabelle hid her son under a bush and covered him with a blanket. Until this moment the babe had been alert, but quiet, for silence was the first thing an Indian infant learned. But suddenly, Little Birch let out a squeal of rage and began to cry loudly.

Terrified for her son's safety, Annabelle leaned close to him and soothed him with soft words of comfort. Almost at once Little Birch stopped crying. Kissing him once on his tiny forehead, Annabelle broke from the timber and raced back across the clearing, circling widely in a calculated gamble to draw the hard-charging Crow warrior away from her son.

The Crow was pleased at the chase, turned his pony, and took after Annabelle happily, uttering short, happy yips as he bore down on her. Just before Annabelle reached the stream, the Crow warrior overtook her. She bent her body protectively as the triumphant warrior circled her, emitting a series of high, shrieking yips. Desperate, Annabelle tried to break past the Crow's pony to the water, but the Crow only laughed and began striking her repeatedly about the head and shoulders with his quirt, driving her to her knees. Then the Crow warrior jumped from his pony and strode toward her, his painted face stark and terrible. Annabelle got to her feet and tried to rush past him, but the Crow caught her easily and held her fast, grinning.

Three mounted Crow's started across the stream toward them. And then, to her horror, she looked beyond the Crow who had her and saw another mounted Crow emerge from the timber holding Little Birch in one hand. Uttering a victory cry, the Crow warrior headed back to the burning Shoshone village with his prize. Screaming, Annabelle tried desperately to break free of the Crow warrior and go after her son.

Impatient with her, Annabelle's captor struck her with his fist, catching her neatly on the point of her jaw. She felt herself spinning to the ground. But no sooner did she hit it than she was up again, storming at the Crow. He punched her again, this time in the stomach. Annabelle doubled over, retching. The Crow slammed her to the ground and with an almost negligent slash of his knife removed a fistful of her scalp and danced gleefully away from her, holding the bloody scalp lock triumphantly aloft while he shouted out his great victory. Annabelle knew enough of the Crow tongue to realize he was telling the three approaching Crows that he had just taken the scalp of the Golden-Haired One, the sister of Golden Hawk, and that soon he would have that warrior's scalp as well.

Blood streaming from the laceration in her scalp became a weight on the side of her head; she felt the warm blood coursing down the side of her face and neck into her bosom. The mounted Crows had reached them by this time and began circling gleefully. Annabelle saw the face of her captor beneath the war paint and for the first time realized he was not much older than sixteen.

The Crow turned his back on Annabelle to grin up at the three circling warriors. He waved Annabelle's scalp lock at them in triumph, and then, to advertise his intent, he dropped his breechclout. Removing the knife from her cleft, Annabelle plunged the long blade into the Crow's back—once, twice, three times. With each thrust she grunted fiercely. The first thrust would have been sufficient, but she was too filled with hatred to stop with only one.

Then she broke past the other astonished Crows and plunged into the stream. After a few strokes she was far enough from the bank to be caught up by the stream's swift current. Once in its icy grip, she was pulled around, then swept swiftly downstream, at times vanishing completely from the sight of the Crows urging their ponies into the swift water after her. But already the swift water was becoming too much for the Indians' ponies. When Annabelle glimpsed them pulling back, she struggled against the current no longer and let herself be pulled along by its sudden, fierce rush, paddling just enough to keep her head above the water.

Soon, she became aware of the roar of the approaching rapids, glimpsing the white, choppy water ahead of her. But glancing back, she saw the Crows racing along the bank after her. She had no choice. It was the rapids or the Crows. Without trying to fight the water's inexorable pull, she allowed herself to be swept into the rapids. She glided swiftly over and between the first smooth rocks. Then the water grew rougher. She did her best to duck past those rocks and boulders she was able to glimpse ahead of her poking above the surface, but she was unable to avoid them all. And as the water slammed her against the boulders, then flung her past, she was battered so fiercely that she almost lost consciousness.

Exhausted, her body so chilled from the icy water that she was gasping for breath, Annabelle felt herself being swept against a high cutbank. She tried to clamber up the steep bank, but the swift water swept her along, until she managed to grab hold of an exposed tree root. She clung to it until she regained her breath and was able to pull herself onto the bank. Running across a small, narrow clearing, she ducked into a stand of cottonwood. Once in its cover, she found refuge behind a large rotting tree trunk, one with its underbrush forming a heavy cover.

A moment later four Crow horsemen pounded along the stream's bank—looking for her, she had no doubt. They vanished downstream, going as far as the waterfall before returning. As they rode back along the embankment, they kept close to the rapids, still searching the swift water for her. Abruptly, they lashed their ponies to a gallop and raced back to the Shoshone village, eager to continue with their killing and pilaging.

Annabelle was reasonably certain the Crow warriors would not return for her. Her scalp taken, her body apparently washed over the falls, the Crows could only assume that they had succeeded in killing Golden Hawk's sister. So for now, at least, she was safe. But what her infant son's fate would be, Annabelle could only guess. Perhaps he would be adopted by a Crow brave. But she had little real hope of this.

For she had listened to Shoshone braves, after returning from similar attacks on Crow or Arap-

aho villages, recount eagerly the many old men
and women they had killed, the screaming in-
fants they had dashed to the ground and trampled in grisly triumph. That such a fate might
already have been visited on Little Birch left
Annabelle cold and dead inside, grief gnawing at
her insides like a small, murderous animal. Resolutely, she thrust away the pain of her loss, lay
her head down on her crossed arms, and fell into
an exhausted sleep.

Annabelle was crying softly when she finished
relating her story. Hawk held her closely, saying
nothing. No words could possibly comfort his
sister for the loss of her son, the death of her
husband—the end of her life as a Shoshone.

They were inside Joe Meek's lodge. Throughout Annabelle's story, Joe Meek had translated
Annabelle's words for Summer Sky in a low,
barely audible undertone. When Annabelle was
done, Summer Sky knew as much as anyone in
the lodge, and her eyes as she gazed now upon
Annabelle revealed an honest and heartfelt com-
passion.

Annabelle wiped her eyes and smiled bravely
at her brother and the others, mumbling an apol-
ogy for her lack of control. The patch taken from
her scalp had been bandaged carefully and she
had combed her long hair over the wound. She
looked haggard. Her face was drawn. Dark circles rimmed her sunken eyes. Her hair still had
gold left in it, however, and as Hawk looked into

his sister's eyes, he saw the steel that had carried her this far, and he knew she would rebound. All she needed was rest and proper nourishment. And time.

Joe Meek spoke up then. "This here feller who found you and brought you in. What'd you say his name was?"

"Captain James Merriwether."

"Captain?"

"He's in the United States Army," Annabelle explained. "He's been scouting the Oregon Territory for his superiors in Washington. It has something to do with Oregon's settlers pressing for statehood, but I didn't understand all of it, even when he did his best to explain it to me."

"I heard of him," said Joe Meek. "He ain't a stranger to these parts. Been out here a year now. A nice-enough gent, full of spit and polish—and a good shot, from what I hear. But he's a greenhorn all the same."

"He was very kind to me," Annabelle said. "I must have looked like a wild animal when I stumbled into his camp, but he treated me like a lady from the very first, even though he knew I'd lived with the Shoshone. It didn't seem to matter to him."

"I'd like to meet him," Hawk said, getting to his feet.

"Then you shall," said Annabelle, also getting up. "James has quarters in the fort and is anxious to meet the famous Golden Hawk." She held up her hand to prevent Hawk from protesting.

"Please, Jed. He said it in such a way I know you won't be offended."

Hawk shrugged. "Then I won't be." He turned to Joe Meek. "Thanks for the hospitality, Joe."

"Yer always welcome, Hawk," Joe Meek replied, getting up quickly. "You two go on out there and meet the captain." He pulled Summer Sky close. "Sky and us won't wait up for you."

As Hawk and Annabelle neared the fort's gate, Hawk felt Annabelle pull up in sudden apprehension.

"What is it?" Hawk asked gently.

"Those Indians over there. Aren't they Crows?"

She was referring to a pocket of seven or eight Crow Indians, handsome and of fine bearing, who had gathered beside the fort's gate. It was evident they had just finished trading for rum—even though it was illegal for the post to sell it to them—and were now dancing about like overgrown kids as they passed the jug around.

"Yes. They're Crow."

Annabelle shuddered. "I hate them."

"You're safe here. They won't give us trouble at this post. It's neutral ground. Besides, there are quite a few soldiers inside."

"Thank God."

They continued on through the gate, and once they had put the Crows behind them, Annabelle spoke up, her voice charged with anger. "I'm sick of them, Jed. Sick to death of them all."

"Them?"

"The aborigines, as James calls them. The Indians. They are so kind and full of love—I know that so well! But then they go mad and kill like sick children. They do terrible things, and they have made me do terrible things as well. Oh, Jed, I must get away from this murderous land and find a measure of civilization, a country where such things cannot happen. Do you know what I mean, Jed?"

"Yes," he said, "I know what you mean."

"Do you remember how surprised you were when I decided to stay with Crow Wing?"

"Yes."

"Would you be surprised now if I told you that all I want is for you to take me back to Kentucky?"

"No," he said, "I am not surprised. Don't you remember? It was a long time ago, but I promised to come after you and do just that."

She hugged his arm and said softly, "Yes, I remember."

"I'm sorry it took me so long."

"Then you will take me back?"

"It's a long way," he said.

"I know that."

"I mean in time as well as place. I don't know anyone in Kentucky, and neither do you. It's been so many years. We don't even know if we've got kin there now."

"I just want to go back."

He pulled her closer and brushed her hair with lips. "Then you shall, sister," he promised. "You shall."

*   *   *

A tall handsome officer in full uniform was striding eagerly across the quadrangle toward them.

"Aha," the officer said to Annabelle, pulling up before them. "I was just coming after you, Miss Annabelle."

"Were you, now?"

"Don't you remember? You promised to introduce me to your brother."

Annabelle turned to Jed. "Jed, may I introduce you to Captain James Merriwether. Captain, my brother, Jed Thompson."

"Also known as Golden Hawk, I understand," said the captain, shaking Hawk's hand warmly. "I am pleased and honored to meet you, sir. There are very few of these aborigines who have not heard of you. You must be some magician, indeed, to have earned such terrible enmity—and respect."

Hawk smiled. "Your servant, sir. I believe I owe you a debt of gratitude. Thank you for helping Annabelle."

"No thanks are necessary, I assure you! It was my pleasure. I count myself fortunate indeed that I was there to assist her. Her tragic story is known to me, and I am proud to know such a courageous woman. You are a lucky man, sir, to have a sister as brave as Annabelle." As he spoke, he smiled warmly at Annabelle and bowed slightly.

Hawk saw Annabelle blush, and for a moment the deep lines, the awful gauntness, went out of her face. In that instant Hawk realized that, as he had surmised, despite the terrible shock of these past weeks, Annabelle remained a strong, vibrant woman—a survivor.

Yes, he would take her back to Kentucky. He already had an excuse—Long Tom's journals, for he had been unable to find an agent he trusted to transport them back East.

Besides, Annabelle was right. It was time to quit this murderous land.

— 11 —

A month later, on a ridge overlooking the Missouri, Hawk, Joe Meek, and Annabelle dismounted and looked down at the palisaded fort that had been built alongside the river. A sprawl of Mandan huts followed the riverbank beyond the fort, and they could see the new river steamboat, *Assiniboin*, being loaded, black wood smoke belching from its twin stacks. They had arrived at Fort Clark in time.

Hawk turned to Joe Meek. "Thanks, Joe. We'll make it from here, all right—I'm sure you can't wait to get back to Brett's Fort and Summer Sky."

"This child ain't gonna say good-bye for good, Hawk. You don't know it yet, but you'll be back. In this here country a man can roam free—and you'll sore miss it when you turn back to them overheated boxes and dismal streets some calls civilization."

171

"I'll miss you, Joe. Give Old Bill a slap on the back for me when you get to Fort Union."

"I'll do that, Hawk."

Joe Meek reached out then and took Annabelle's hand in his and said good-bye to her with a gentleness and a dignity that brought tears to her eyes. Then he mounted up, booted his horse around, and galloped off quickly, his pack horse rearing unhappily at the suddenness of the departure.

Hawk and Annabelle watched him go, then mounted up again and moved on down the slope toward the fort. An hour later they clattered out onto the loading dock. The passengers had not yet gone aboard, and as Hawk and Annabelle rode up, their pack horses in tow, Hawk saw the captain, who was standing on the dock alongside stacked bales of beaver skins, talking to a black roustabout.

Hawk and Annabelle had long since caught their attention. As soon as Hawk and Annabelle began to dismount in front of them, the roustabout left the captain and boarded the steamboat. Hawk helped Annabelle from her saddle, then turned to the ship's captain and introduced himself. He gave his name as Jed Thompson, his sister as Annabelle, then asked if he and Annabelle might book passage on his steamboat.

Under his hat, the captain's hair was snow-white, as were his mustache and his neatly trimmed chin whiskers. He shook Hawk's hand, then smiled cordially at Annabelle, "I am Captain Jeremy Bentham," he said. "And I am delighted to welcome you and your brother aboard." He turned to Hawk then. "How far are you going?"

"Saint Louis first, then Kentucky."

"Kentucky, is it? I have kin there too, young man."

Hawk grinned. "We hope we still have kin there, too. We've been away a long while."

A happy shout came from the shore. Turning, Hawk and Annabelle saw an astonished and delighted Captain James Merriwether hastening along the bank to the loading dock to greet them.

For a full day now, the *Assiniboin* had been steaming down the Missouri, Captain Bentham cautiously navigating the treacherous shoals and sandbars that made the downriver trip so dangerous this time of year. It was evening, but there was still plenty of light from the incandescent moon.

Hawk, Annabelle, and Merriwether were seated on deck in lounge chairs, enjoying the warm southerly breeze. In its bright silver cloak the shoreline was mysterious and hauntingly beautiful.

"Tell me more about these manuscripts of Long Tom's," Merriwether continued eagerly, taking out a small cigar and lighting up. "You've told me a little, but I am most anxious to hear more."

"The first thing to remember," Hawk told him, "is that Long Tom was a Harvard professor and his real name was Algernon Percival Farrington the third."

Merriwether laughed shortly. "Well, I can certainly see why he preferred Long Tom."

"And he *was* long," Hawk continued. "Over six feet tall, and as lanky as a rake handle. But that doesn't matter. I've read much of his journals this past month, and they are fascinating."

"I can iamgine," said Merriwether. "Not only is this country beautiful, Jed, but for a trained scientist—whether he be a botanist, zoologist, or a geologist—these mountains are a wonderland, an unending garden of earthly delights. I am sure there is much in Farrington's journals that will be of tremendous value to the scientific community, and to the general public as well."

"That's why I'm bringing them back."

"And of course you promised him you would, Jed," Merriwether reminded him. "That's certainly a large part of it, is it not?"

"Of course."

"Don't forget me, Jed," Annabelle said. "You promised to take me back to Kentucky."

Merriwether looked warmly at Annabelle, concern etched on his long, handsome face. "I suppose you have had enough of this country, Annabelle."

"Yes," she agreed solemnly, "I have."

"You know, I was thinking. The story of your capture and escape would make a quite fascinating novel."

"I suppose it would. But someone else would have to write it. I have no desire to dwell on what has happened to me. It has been a nightmare, and I want only to forget it . . . completely."

He leaned closer to her, concern etched on his face. "Perhaps you'll feel differently, once you've let time heal your wounds."

"Perhaps," she said, her lips now a firm, hard line. "But if you don't mind, I would prefer you to drop the subject."

"Of course," Merriwether said, seeing how upset Annabelle was. "It was stupid of me to bring it up. I apologize."

Annabelle reached out quickly and took his hand. "There is no need for you to apologize."

A pleasant young married couple they had been introduced to at the captain's table that noon strolled by. Like them, the couple was admiring the moonlit shoreline, chattering pleasantly as they approached. Within a few feet of Hawk and Annabelle, however, they abruptly stopped talking, looked straight ahead, and walked on past, deliberately ignoring Hawk and his sister.

Hawk heard Merriwether's greeting die in his throat. When the couple was out of earshot, Hawk glanced angrily at Merriwether. "Nice couple, that."

Annabelle looked considerably subdued, her color, so robust of late, had gone pale.

It was obvious why the couple had chosen to ignore their presence on the deck. They had decided that Annabelle and Jed were little better than savages, for in his enthusiasm Merriwether had excitedly recounted to the captain and the others at the table that noon as many of their marvelous adventures as he could recall. The shocked silence that fell over the table alerted him—too late—to his mistake.

"It's my fault," said Merriwether miserably. "My big mouth led to that. Will you ever forgive me, Annabelle?"

"I do wish you would stop asking me to forgive you, James. It is most unbecoming, I assure you. You have nothing for which to apologize."

With that she got to her feet and started for her cabin. Hawk wanted to follow and offer Annabelle some comfort, but Merriwether was after his sister like an unleashed whippet. Hawk watched him go, a slight smile on his face. He was sure Merriwether would be able to comfort Annabelle. He had not been doing badly up until now, at any rate.

Hawk got up and moved off in the other direction, trying to shake the unpleasantness that clung to him since that crude rebuff he and Annabelle had suffered. It should not have bothered him. What did he care about these people? But it did bother him because of what it had done to Annabelle.

So far, Annabelle's recovery had been nothing short of remarkable. A hairpiece she had fashioned from her own ample locks now completely covered the small hole in her scalp. A doctor at Fort Hall had assured her that the scalp wound would close up still more, though it would never do so completely, leaving at the most a circle of pure skull bone the size of a silver dollar. But no more. Annabelle had told Hawk she was perfectly willing to live with that.

Meanwhile, with good food Annabelle had filled out, and long hours of sleep had done the rest, banishing the dark circles under her eyes and restoring the bloom to her cheeks. It was no wonder, Hawk realized, that Captain James Merriwether was so attentive.

"Hello, Mr. Thompson."

Hawk turned to see a woman the captain had introduced to him a few hours ago. Her name was Estelle Van Diver, and she had seemed quite anxious to meet him. Her manner made him uncomfortable, however, and he had hastened to break away from her and her husband, a little fellow who followed after her like an unhappy puppy waiting to be petted. He was not pleased now to find her approaching him, though she was very beautiful, in an icy, aloof manner. She had a high forehead, a long, graceful neck and hazel eyes that seemed to blaze out at him.

"Hello, Mrs. Van Diver."

"You remember my name. How nice! Please, do call me Estelle. I am sure we are going to be very good friends."

"Why?"

"You are a man, aren't you? I have heard all about you—and your fabulous adventures among the aborigines."

It was a conversation Hawk did *not* wish to continue. But Estelle, laughing lightly, took his arm and pulled him eagerly on down the deck, heading for her cabin. "I insist! You must tell me all about it. Let's go into my cabin, where we can be more comfortable."

Estelle's husband appeared, hurrying toward them. When he saw Estelle with Hawk, the little man's face sort of caved in. Hawk pulled free of Estelle's grasp.

"I thought you were at the tables," Estelle demanded angrily as her husband got closer.

"I'm sorry, dear," he said, pulling up before her unhappily, "but I needed a fresh deck of cards."

"Then get them," she snapped.

Nodding, Alfred Van Diver stepped past them into his cabin. As he did so, he glanced apologetically at Hawk. "I—I'm sorry," he said.

"No need to be," said Hawk, moving off quickly, grateful to be out of Estelle Van Diver's clutches.

The moon was high enough for Hawk to see the shore almost as clearly as if it were day. Peering more closely at the apparition, he was certain his eyes were not playing tricks on him. A huge gray timber wolf was padding along the embankment, floating along on ghostly feet, moving so effortlessly it seemed to be floating over the ground. Up steep bluffs it bounded, then down the other side, every now and then vanishing for long stretches into patches of timber, but reappearing each time still abreast of the steamer, its loping, ground-devouring trot undiminished.

With a growing sense of unease, Hawk watched the wolf. He recalled Running Moon's last words —her terrified warning about Wolf Heart. A chill ran up his spine. He could not believe Running Moon's fear of Wolf Heart was anything more than an overwrought, superstitious dread of a powerful and feared medicine man. And yet . . .

The wolf vanished as suddenly as it had appeared.

Hawk peered intently at the moonlit banks,

the sand hills, the clumps of willow and cottonwood, the river's black water, searching for any
sign of the wolf. But it was gone. Its game, whatever it had been, was over for now.

Hawk left the railing, attempting to shake off
the uneasiness that still clung to him, and headed
for his cabin. Rounding a corner, he found Wolf
Heart standing by the railing. River water poured
off him, sending a steady stream across the deck.
He was armed only with his knife and a hatchet.
His bow was on his back. On his face was a cruel
smile. In the darkness, his eyes glowed like coals
from the middle of hell.

Hawk did not want to believe what his senses
told him.

"Ah! The mighty Golden Hawk is fleeing,"
Wolf Heart taunted.

"I am fleeing no one. I am taking my sister
back to her people."

"It is the same thing. Your medicine is good no
more in the Blackfoot land. You run from the
medicine of Wolf Heart. You are craven, Golden
Hawk."

"Why do you pursue me?"

"You and your settlers have sent many of my
band's chiefs to the Sandhills. My magic was not
at Brett's Fort to save them, or they would be
with the living now. So I come for you. I challenge you. Once you gave me my life. But I have
given you your life in return. So now it is time to
settle matters between us. Meet me in fair combat. Allow me to avenge the death of my chiefs."

"No."

"The milk of cows flows in your veins—not blood."

"Taunt me all you want. It does not matter."

"Does it matter that I sent the grizzly that killed Running Moon?"

Hawk stared at Wolf Heart. It could not be true what Wolf Heart was saying. On the other hand, how did Hawk know Wolf Heart was *not* telling the truth? Astonishment grew in him, then anger, deep-running and fierce, galvanizing him. Could this wily medicine man possibly be capable of such feats? Had Running Moon seen clearly when she insisted the wolf she had fired upon had really been Wolf Heart?

At that moment Hawk realized there was only one way for him to be sure. "At the next landing," Hawk told Wolf Heart, "I will disembark. You will have your fair combat, if that is possible with one such as you."

Wolf Heart smiled. "With Golden Hawk I shall fight as one warrior fights another. It will be enough for him. The medicine of Golden Hawk has no power over him."

Wolf Heart stepped up onto the railing, then dived off.

At the railing Hawk watched the Blood warrior swim through the dark waters, clamber up onto the shore, and disappear into the night.

— 12 —

Annabelle was no longer crying. She stood close by Merriwether and his hand was about her waist. The strength he was giving Annabelle was making the farewell bearable for her, and for this Hawk was profoundly grateful.

"Are you sure—absolutely sure?" Annabelle asked one more time. "Do you really have to go back to that . . . dark land?"

"Yes."

"Oh, Jed, why?"

He had already told her, but he owed her all the patience it was in his power to give. "I don't like the civilization this steamer is heading for, or the people in it. Joe Meek was right. He said I'd be coming back, and I am."

"Not everyone is like the people on this boat."

"Enough of them are, Annabelle."

She took a deep breath, then looked up at Merriwether, her glance imploring him to say something, anything, that might persuade Hawk to remain on the boat.

"I do wish you would continue on with us, Jed," Merriwether said sincerely. Then he paused and said resolutely, "But I understand that a man must do what he must do and go where his spirit leads him. It is as simple as that."

"Yes," Hawk said, grateful that Merriwether understood. "That's about it."

"Don't worry about Annabelle. I will take good care of her. As soon as we reach Saint Louis, we will be married, then we shall journey to Kentucky to find your kin."

"I thank you for that."

Annabelle took a deep breath. In that instant, it seemed, she came to accept Hawk's decision. Brightening somewhat, she said, "And we'll see to it that Long Tom's journals get properly published. James has promised me that."

The steamboat's whistle piped up shrilly, impatiently. Hawk saw the captain in the wheelhouse standing at the railing. They waved at each other. Stepping forward then, Hawk shook Merriwether's hand, after which he pulled Annabelle to him and hugged her for a long moment, almost squeezing the life out of her. Then he stepped back, trying not to see the fresh tears coursing down Annabelle's cheeks.

"Now get back to that steamboat, you two," he told them roughly, his voice momentarily betraying him.

Turning, he hurried off the dock toward the small trading post. When he reached the crest of the embankment, he turned. The steamboat was pulling away from the landing, its paddle wheels churning the water into a white froth. Annabelle and Merriwether were on the deck facing the shore, waving.

Hawk waved once in return, then headed for the trading post. There were horses to purchase and lead balls and powder for his Hawken—and a battle with a pure devil still before him.

For seven days Hawk followd the Missouri River north, pushing deeper and deeper into Blackfoot country without once catching sight of Wolf Heart. There were no tracks—no sign of any kind—to indicate that the Indian was near. Hawk pressed on nevertheless, certain that when the time and the occasion suited him, Wolf Heart would make his presence known.

On the eighth day, about midmorning, Hawk glimpsed the same large timber wolf he had seen from the boat deck. It was peering at him from a ridge not a hundred yards distant. Hawk pulled his mount up and yanked his Hawken from its sling. He had already primed it, but when he checked the firing cap and looked up, the wolf had vanished. He sat his horse awhile, peering around at the timber and rocks, waiting for the wolf to reappear. But it did not, and after a few minutes Hawk dropped his rifle back into its sling, tugged his pack animal around, and urged his horse onward.

That evening, Hawk made a dry camp in deep timber, chewed a few strips of jerky, then hoisted himself into a tall pine. When he had reached the topmost limb, one capable of supporting no more than his weight, he tied himself to the branch and slept. He was awakened close to dawn by someone shaking the tree. Looking down, he saw Wolf Heart staring up at him about twenty feet from the tree. The pine was at least six feet in diameter. How in hell, he wondered, had Wolf Heart managed to shake the tree enough to wake him?

"It is morning, Golden Hawk," Wolf Heart called up to him. "Turn into the Great Cannibal Owl and fly down. I am waiting for you."

Hawk looked around for the wolf, but did not see him. "It won't take me long," Hawk called.

Untying himself, Hawk clambered down the tree. But when he dropped at last to the forest floor, he found that Wolf Heart had vanished. He checked the ground where the Indian had been standing. There were no tracks, not a sign that anything or anyone had stood there.

Hawk felt his mouth go dry and the hair on the back of his neck rose slightly.

Two days later, as Hawk pushed on through a clump of alders, he glanced across the stream he was following and saw Wolf Heart perched on a log. Hawk halted his mount. Wolf Heart stood up and beckoned to him.

Hawk plunged his horse into the stream, his eagerness to end this business with Wolf Heart causing him to act rashly. Shallow though the water appeared to be at this point, Hawk's horse was suddenly in over its head, swimming desperately to cut through a current much swifter than it could manage. Hawk hung on as best he could while he untied his pack horse's lead. The overtaxed pack horse made a futile but gallant effort to gain the far shore, but the last Hawk saw of it, the horse was spinning helplessly as it vanished around a bend.

Hawk's own horse was swimming strongly now, stretched to its full length, its snout well out of the water, its tail floating straight out behind it. When Hawk reached the shore, he lashed the horse up onto the embankment and found that once again Wolf Heart had vanished.

Hawk pulled up, furious with himself. He was out one pack horse and the gear it had carried.

That night, on the side of a broad mountain flank, he built up a roaring campfire and sat by it, waiting. He could have gone up into a tree, as usual, but it was time for him to remain on solid ground and meet his nemesis. Hawk finished his coffee and jerky and was taking out his clay pipe when Wolf Heart stepped out of the darkness beyond the fire and came to a halt, his arms folded. Putting aside his pipe and picking up his already primed rifle, Hawk stood up.

He would kill this son of a bitch with one shot—no fancy sparring around. All he wanted was to get this madness over with. Stepping wide of the fire, Hawk brought up his rifle and closed his finger over the trigger. Wolf Heart remained immobile, his powerful arms still folded calmly over his chest.

Again Hawk found himself peering into this savage Blood's eyes—and once more found himself hesitant to kill the man in cold blood. Was Wolf Heart right? Did Hawk's backbone lack iron? Was it true that he could not kill a man into whose soul he was peering? Deliberately, Hawk leveled the barrel on Wolf Heart's chest. If this medicine man had any tricks, Hawk told himself grimly, he'd better use them now.

Wolf Heart did.

A powerful blow struck Hawk from behind and slammed him brutally forward. Turning his head, Hawk saw it was the large timber wolf, its hot breath searing his face and neck. As Hawk hit the ground, his rifle discharged, the ball slamming harmlessly into the forest floor. Rolling over, he flung up his left arm to protect himself from the wolf's snapping teeth. The growling that came from deep within the animal's throat was enough to chill his blood, but even more terrifying were the beast's cold, intent eyes, the scalding heat of its breath, and its terrible eagerness to get at Hawk's throat. This was the same wolf Hawk had struggled with before, he realized, but this time there would be no Running Moon to help beat it off.

Watching from a safe distance was Wolf Heart, smiling grimly as he waited for his wolf to reduce to bloody shreds the great Golden Hawk. But Hawk still had his sheathed bowie. With a desperate heave, he shoved his forearm deep into the wolf's mouth, sending it onto his back. Then he flung himself forward onto the wolf's belly, wrapping both legs around the animal's thighs in a hellish embrace. Forcing the wolf's head to extend out past his left shoulder, Hawk tucked his own head in behind the wolf's. The wolf struggled to turn its head far enough to crunch into the back of Hawk's neck, and Hawk could hear the wolf's teeth clicking furiously.

Drawing his bowie, Hawk plunged it into the wolf's back. Twice he stabbed the wolf, probing for the spinal column. The wolf cried out in sharp, piteous yelps. Wolf Heart rushed forward to save it. But the Indian was too late as Hawk's third and final stroke severed the wolf's spinal chord.

Flinging the wolf aside, Hawk jumped up to meet Wolf Heart's charge. Bending slightly, he waited, his bloody blade held in readiness, strips of torn flesh hanging from his left forearm.

But the Indian pulled up hastily and halted.

"I'm waiting, Wolf Heart," Hawk taunted, sucking in deep gutfulls of air. "Maybe now we will be just two warriors fighting to the death, with no magic on either side."

But Wolf Heart had apparently lost all enthusiasm for the showdown he had pleaded for on the steamboat. The great timber wolf had been Wolf Heart's secret medicine, in his eyes a magical extension of himself. But now the wolf lay torn and lifeless on the ground before him, leaving Wolf Heart naked before the world. And there was nothing more pitiable than an Indian convinced his medicine had lost its power.

Wolf Heart turned and fled.

Hawk wanted to let him go, but he knew he could not do that. He had to finish off Wolf Heart now while he had the chance—or he would be forever watching and waiting for this vengeful Blackfoot to step out of ambush and kill him.

Snatching up his rifle, Hawk raced after Wolf Heart, stopping every now and then to listen for the noise the panicked Indian made in his flight through the dark woods. He overtook the Indian finally and saw him racing across a moonlit clearing. Hawk raised his rifle, tracked the running figure coolly, and fired. Wolf Heart stumbled and fell, got up, and vanished into the timber beyond the clearing.

Satisfied he had winged Wolf Heart at least, Hawk trotted doggedly after him. Wolf Heart was moving much slower now, and Hawk rapidly closed the distance between them. When finally he overtook the fleeing Indian, it was on the brink of a steep gorge, and Wolf Heart was frantically picking his way down its precipitous side. Hawk peered down. In his haste Wolf Heart was dislodging stones and boulders into the black gorge below.

Hawk waited, his reata's noose opened wide. Then he saw the wounded Indian's bloody shoulder as the man leaned out to pick his way farther down the steep slope. Hawk dropped the noose over Wolf Heart's head, then snapped it shut and yanked hard, swinging the Indian out over the gorge. There was only a short cry as the noose throttled Wolf Heart. Glancing down, Hawk saw the Indian's lifeless form swinging in the void.

He wound the reata a couple of times around the base of a piñon, then knotted it securely. He was in Blood country now. Soon enough a Blackfoot warrior would find Wolf Heart hanging from Hawk's reata—and would know at once who had finished off the famous Blood medicine man.

And that was what Hawk wanted.

A week later, in order to replace his lost pack horse, Hawk slipped a fine war pony from its picket in front of a famous Blood chief's lodge and was at least ten miles from the chief's village before dawn broke and his theft could be discovered. He felt enormous satisfaction. His years with the Comanches had taught him well.

He lived off the land for another week, his Hawken finding much fresh game. When he reached the northern fringe of Crow country and found himself at last in sight of Brett's Fort, he pulled up and dismounted, built a fire, and lit his pipe, puffing solemnly as he tried to get things clear in his head finally.

Perhaps he was deviling himself for nothing. The wagon train might already have left for South Pass. The settlers could not wait for him forever, especially if the other wagon train had already joined them; and he had not given much of a promise to Kathleen. She had made more of it than she should have. Furthermore, there could be no doubt that John Barley would be more than anxious to set off without Hawk.

Earlier, convinced he would never again set foot on these hills again, Hawk had tried to talk

Joe Meek into scouting for the wagon train, but Joe Meek had been determined to take Summer Sky north with him and join Old Bill Williams for the coming winter. Joe Meek was no fool. He had known for sure what kind of a welcome Summer Sky would receive from the settlers.

Well, there really was no choice. He would go on to Brett's Fort. If Angus MacLennan and his fiery sister were still there waiting for him, he would do his best to scout for them.

There was no chance at all that he would return to that valley he shared for a brief, happy while with Running Moon. Indeed, there never could be such a valley for him ever again. He had been trying to escape the human race in that valley—but for him there could be no such escape. He was born for strife, not tranquillity. And besides, he too was human. Though this kowledge filled him at times with pure despair, it was a burden all men shared.

More important—and this was something he had been considering since he left the steamboat—perhaps he could do what Long Tom had done. He could write down his own account of this land. When he was gone, his journals would remain an accurate record of his adventures in this fierce land and of the children from hell who inhabited it. It would be a legacy for those who would come after him, for Annabelle perhaps and the children who would bless her union with Captain James Merriwether.

Feeling a little better, Hawk emptied his pipe, and mounted up. An hour later he rode into

Brett's Fort and saw the many covered wagons on the verge of pulling out for Oregon Territory. Angus MacLennan and Kathleen hurried eagerly toward him, their faces wreathed in smiles at his sudden, unexpected appearance.

Hawk smiled too. For a few months at least, this rambling wagon train snaking over the mountains would be his home.